The Ghost Show

Irvine Hunt

The Ghost Show is Irvine Hunt's second novel and is the follow-on adventure to *The Drover's Boy*. When he was seven he wrote an exercise book full of poems and an excited aunty said *Oh*, and took them to show a publisher. The poems were never seen again.

At twenty he became a reporter on the *Accrington Observer*, then a sub-editor on the *Western Morning News*; five years in Fleet Street on the foreign desk of *The Daily Telegraph*, and finally the *Cumberland News*. He lived in Norway and Sweden for two years and walked round Spain and Portugal for seven months. Between times he lectured for the British Film Institute about the beginnings and origins of the moving cinema.

info@irvinehunt.co.uk

Other books by Irvine Hunt:

The Drover's Boy. *Handstand Press*
Norman Nicholson's Lakeland. *Robert Hale*
Lakeland Yesterday. *Vol I: Smith-Settle; Vol II, Waltersgill*
Manlaff and Toewoman. *Rusland Press*
The Lakeland Pedlar. *Pinewood Publications.*

E-book editions:
Dating the Witch, (short stories)
Cub Reporter: The Accrington Observer
Wild Runaways

The Ghost Show

Irvine Hunt

HANDSTAND PRESS

Published by Handstand Press
East Banks, Dent, Sedbergh. Cumbria LA10 5QT
www.handstandpress.co.uk

First Published in 2014

Cover design by Sophie Bennett
Map and projection drawings by Pete Langley
Designed and set by Russell Holden, Pixel Tweaks. Ulverston
Printed in Great Britain by Short Run Press, Exeter, Devon

ISBN: 978-0-9576609-2-2

For Christian and Maisie and Shiloh

Thank you

Many friends, acquaintances and experts have given help with *The Ghost Show* and to them all I offer my thanks, and especially to my publisher Liz Nuttall. Among those who have given sound advice are Ross and Josie Baxter, Fiona Cox, Lucilla Laval, Suki Pay, Lorraine Quince of Annan Museum; Harry Fancy, former curator of Whitehaven Museum; Claire Winter-Moore, The Beacon Museum, Whitehaven; Joanne Turner, Dumfries Museum; and the staff at libraries in Carlisle, Cockermouth, Penrith, Workington and at the British Library in London.

Help came from many fairground organ, harmonium, limelight and old-projector specialists. Eminent among them is Richard Dean of Dean Organs in Bristol who in an amazing coincidence, in an engaging parallel story to *The Ghost Show*, is part-way through composing a musical based on the early days of cinema, and which one day I hope many of us will hear.

Others who have helped include Fred Stone of the Musical Museum; George Dawson, Victor Saddle, Jim Hawkins; Rory Cook, collections information officer, The Science Museum; Clive Polden, the Cinema Theatre Association Archive; Maurice Thornton, The Curzon Community Cinema; and Andrew Youdell, of the British Film Institute.

At the film institute many young hopeful filmmakers and writers were taught by John Huntley, the brilliant film historian, whose enthusiasm inspired us about the excitement of the origins and beginnings of the cinema.

Contents

1

Poster Boys

Billy Wilson hurried round Keswick, anxious not to be noticed. Another mizzling morning was creeping down off the fells. It had rained on and off for days and once more he was soaked through under his old mackintosh. Despite the wet, his supply of Ghost Show posters was dry enough. A dozen were rolled up inside his shoulder bag along with a pot of glue and a paintbrush. It was his yearly task, always at a rush, always out of breath.

It took him an hour to poster the town. He stuck the first on a fence by the railway station. A second went up on the door of the Moot Hall, and a third, before anyone saw him, on top of two other notices on a church notice board. Billy worked warily. The police were not keen on young lads sticking posters all over the place. But by mid-morning the job was done. All twelve were up and he hurried home.

Miles away in Cockermouth another boy, Ernie Carver, was starting a similar run. And on the Cumberland coast a third whose name few could pronounce (it was Wjeksaou) was sticking up a whole lot more of the Ghost Show adverts in the little steel town of Workington.

While these boys were at work, away to the north a line of fairground wagons was rumbling down through the showers towards them, the drivers slumped in their seats, seemingly asleep as they overlooked their plodding horses. The convoy of wagons was intent on reaching Carlisle in time to start a busy week of fairs.

As the wagons passed through each small town people braved the weather and came out of houses and shops to watch them go past. Excited youngsters pointed at the biggest wagon. "The ghosts is in that un! They chain 'em up!"

Their mothers told them not to be silly and to stop talking nonsense. It was only a fairground show – and everyone knew that ghosts did not exist. Yet that was strange because many of the mothers and fathers in the past had seen the ghosts too and were unable to explain what they had seen, except that somehow it had been scaring.

The line of caravans slowed as it struggled up a long hill. One by one they crossed the brow and then the teams of horses set off down the other side at a quicker pace. All knew they must arrive in Carlisle by Saturday in time for the first of the fairs. Everyone was praying for better weather. Distant thunder rumbled along the horizon. The ghosts were on their way.

2

Into The Wind

The boy was pedalling hard and finding it tough going. He was tired of the wind. Tired of the showers. His battered bike was squeaking. His right knee was hurting. It was three in the afternoon and the old Cumberland road was full of potholes. In short, Henry Hodgekin was feeling sorry for himself and wishing he had put off cycling to Carlisle until tomorrow.

Solemn-faced Ted Liddle had told him the bad news at the breakfast table days earlier.

"Annie and me's been thinking things over. We've farmed here in Fingland nearly all our lives but we've decided to sell up. We're calling it a day."

Henry was dismayed. He had worked as a farm lad for the Liddles for two years. He had noticed this past few months how Ted was finding the work harder going, but selling up still came as a shock.

Henry's gloom touched the old man. "We're sorry, lad." The farmer glanced sympathetically. "You're a good worker but I know getting a job isn't easy."

"Nay, I'll be all right," said Henry. "I'll go and see mum and I'll find summat."

But deep down he was feeling sad. It wasn't just his job he was losing, that was going to be hard enough; he was losing two people he cared for: Ted and Annie were like a second family. Somehow without anything being said Henry had come to rely on Ted, perhaps because he still missed his own dad of long ago.

"It'll be the hirings soon," said Ted. "I'm thinking you'll likely get summat there."

The hirings were not a reassuring thought but Henry kept that to himself. It might be the only way to get a job. It was a bad year. Everyone knew lots of men and women were struggling to find work.

The farmer felt in a pocket and pulled out a small packet. "This is for you from Annie and me. But don't you be opening it yet!"

Henry stammered his thanks. He felt at the packet. Something fat and heavy was wrapped inside.

"Be sure you don't drop it," said Ted.

"I won't," Henry promised. He paused as if to say more but he didn't know how to say it. It was just he was going to miss them.

And that's how it happened. Everything in Henry's life was changing; he'd packed his old canvas bag with a few belongings and strapped it on the back of the bike; he'd been over to see his mother at Fingland and told her he was off to find a job, and now the most important thing was to get to the hirings in Carlisle and find work.

Head down against the wind. Crumpled flannel trousers tucked in his socks, jacket buttoned. Lean bodied but not frail. Even so, the wind a real struggle, buffeting him about the road. Winded, he came to a halt and flopped down on the grass verge while he got his breath.

He had never been to the hirings but everyone knew what happened. You stood in the street with others all around you and you waited until a farmer looked you over, and if he took you on, you worked for him for half a year, sometimes longer. If one farmer didn't want you then you just had to hope the next one would. Henry knew it was a gamble. `

He got out the packet for another look. Ted shouldn't have! It was a fob watch. Henry marvelled. It had a dark blue inlay, the kind every lad worth his salt dreamed of owning. He would always keep it.

The jingling of a bell made him look up. Back along the road a bulky looking contraption was coming round a bend. It was another bike, but quite unlike his own Swift. A deep pannier basket was bracketed over a small front wheel, with a bigger wheel behind. Henry recognised it was a butcher's delivery bike.

The boy in the seat jammed on the brakes as he saw Henry, then almost immediately tipped over sideways.

"Ow! Help!"

The boy landed with a spectacular crunch on the road.

Henry hurried across.

"Crikey, you all right?"

The boy struggled up, wheezing badly.

"Blooming thing's too big!"

Between them they hauled the machine upright.

"Are you a butcher's boy?"

The boy was thin faced and had a ragged mop of hair.

"Am I heck." He lowered his voice. "I pinched it."

"Blimey!"

Henry shot a glance back along the road.

"It was the old geezer's next door, back in Keswick. But he don't use it no more, and I gotta get ta Carlisle."

"That's where I'm going."

"Yeah, well, it's ruddy hard work. I've been pedalling all morning."

The boy wiped his hands down his pants. "Me dad's dead mad at me 'cause I quit the wood yard. He told me to get some brains! Sadie, that's his new girl friend, she said it was best thing I could do – get a new job, I mean."

Henry eyed the boy. He was a real titch with a gap in his front teeth. Apart from boots and socks, all he seemed to have on was a shabby grey jersey and short pants.

"So where you stopping?" asked Henry.

"Dunno. I'll get summat." The boy smirked. "I'm right good at finding places."

"If you want to come with me you gonna have to keep up," Henry warned.

"Easy. I can keep up with anyone."

Henry wasn't impressed. The lad sounded cocky.

"What they call you?"

"Snivel . . . Sniv for short."

"Sniv? What sort of name's that?"

"It's 'cause I get colds."

He gave a hefty sniff to prove it.

They looked at his bike. The chain had come off.

"It's useless," said Snivel.

But Henry was good with his fingers and got it back on.

They set off together, the wind as strong as ever.

Despite his boast, half a mile later Snivel had to get down. He was looking pale. "It's me breath. I get the wheezes."

Henry groaned. He had guessed this would happen.

They were at the edge of a wood.

"Oh, yes! And where might you be a-going?"

The voice took them by surprise.

A mound of stones lay piled up near the road and behind it sat an old man in a floppy hat. He was feeding twigs into a fire.

"Don't want ta speak ta Charlie, eh?"

"We didn't see you," said Henry, then remembering the question: "We're going to Carlisle."

"Ha, is ya now!"

The man's face crinkled. Hammers lay on the ground and Henry realised he was a stonebreaker, making stone for the roads.

The man lifted a kettle off the flames. "Well sit down, sit down, if you're wanting a brew don't be standing there."

He poured mugs of black tea, pulled out a stout knife and cut each of them a thick slice of apple pie.

"So you isn't Keswick lads?"

"He is," said Henry. "I'm from Fingland, at a farm, where me mum works. We're going to the hirings to get us jobs."

"Is ya now? Niver bin ta Carlisle, not in forty years."

"You must have," said Henry, surprised.

"Charlie don't like town folk. Nowt but troublemakers. I'd give Carlisle a miss if it was me."

It was warm beside the fire as they talked and they were sorry when the roadman knocked out his pipe on a stone and poured the tea dregs onto the flames. He wrapped the rest of the pie in a piece of newspaper. This he handed to Henry.

"Go on. Take it. The missis gives me plenty."

Snivel watched and for some reason he looked uncomfortable.

"You mind them townies," the man called as they left.

The wind was as bad as ever. Snivel struggled with the cumbersome bike and in the end Henry changed over and rode it himself.

Snivel said: "What place you stoppin in?"

Henry had worked that out. "There's a shed place behind a pub. I slept there once."

"Oh, yeah." They continued in silence when Snivel suddenly inquired: "Hey, do ya like girls?"

"What?"

"I've had some beauties." Snivel smirked. "Marigold, me last 'un. She'd do owt for me. She used ta mend me socks."

Henry didn't answer immediately. "I've got a girl, at least, not exactly . . ."

In fact, he hadn't. Jenny was working at her aunt's farm at Fingland when they first met, a slim girl in a pale blue dress. He had been attracted to her at once but had never said anything. A moment came one evening when he almost kissed her. But he dithered and a day later he was miffed to find she had left her aunt's without saying a word. Well she could go for all he cared. Not that he was going to tell this titch.

They pedalled slowly, glad to be on the move again but hardly a mile had passed and the butcher's bike lurched to one side. Henry, taken by surprise, struggled to get off.

"Of all the rotten luck!"

The front tyre had gone flat. Henry examined it and found a split in the rubber.

"It's worn out! You got any patches?"

Snivel shook his head. Neither had Henry.

In a gloomy mood they set off, pushing both bikes. Bit by bit the punctured tyre shredded until the wheel began to grate on the rims.

Henry, exasperated, changed tactics. He dragged the machine into a field and dumped it in long grass behind a tumbled barn.

"Someone'll find it."

They set off again as rain began to fall. Snivel tried balancing on the crossbar of the Swift as Henry pedalled. But it was hard going and at times they took turns to wheel the bike instead of riding. An hour later they reached the outskirts of Carlisle. Neither of them knew that their adventures were about to begin.

3

Job Hunt

Jenny was as ready as she could be. A holiday in Keswick at cousin Alice's was over. She had brushed her hair so that it hung down her back in a tidy tress. Her button boots were shining, and she was wearing her good grey coat.

Nine o'clock was striking on the Moot Hall clock in the town centre as the two girls arrived in the market place.

"The register office isn't posh," said Alice. "But it's better than nowt."

Jenny smiled excitedly. "It's all right, but I want somewhere good! A doctor's family if I can get it." She was determined to change her life. Now that she was fourteen a maid's job at a doctor's would be a good first step.

The office was a converted shop with a window full of notices.

"Biddall's Ghosts!" said Alice, reading. "Do ya want to see a ghost? Oh, here we are."

Under the ghost show advert a card announced:

> *Miss A. Bewley*
> *Respectfully Intimates*
> *she has Opened a High-class*
> *REGISTER OFFICE*
> *FOR DOMESTIC SERVANTS*
> *Market Place, Keswick*

Alice peered through a gap in the adverts. "Come on. We'll find you a nice rich doctor, with a glass eye and a lovely wax moustache!" Jenny laughed, but the joke was short-lived. They stepped inside and found that the high-class office in fact was dismal and shabby. A large breasted woman in a shapeless grey dress and a hairy chin sat behind a desk.

She definitely looked like a Miss Bewley, thought Jenny.

"A doctor's family?" said Miss Bewley. She shifted her position and made sure she sounded surprised. "I don't think so. It's your first time here? Well I have nothing available, especially not at a doctor's. Everybody's chasing jobs these days."

"So I am wasting my time," said Jenny wondering why the office had bothered to open. She moved as if to leave.

At once Miss Bewley seemed to have a change of heart.

"No, wait . . . as it happens I have a client coming in this morning. If you sit next door, there's a small chance – but I can't promise anything."

It didn't sound hopeful but Jenny decided she would wait.

Alice sat with her in a shadowy side room and it was almost eleven o'clock before they heard the doorbell sound.

A small thin-faced woman came in. She was dressed entirely in black as if widowed. She looked round the office and walked past Miss Bewley.

"I presume you are seeking a place?" she demanded of Jenny.

Jenny, startled by the woman's abrupt manner, nodded that she was. "I'm wanting to work for a doctor's family."

"Is that so?"

Miss Bewley struggled up from her seat. "Good morning, Miss Stalker, how may we help you?"

"I'm not sure you can," said Miss Stalker. "That last girl you got me was useless. I am surprised you sent her to me, a slattern of a girl, nothing was cleaned properly."

She turned and fixed her eyes on Jenny. "And what makes you think you are good enough to work for a doctor?"

"I'm good around the house and . . ."

The woman gave a grim smile. "Lots of young girls are good round the house. Doctor's aren't the only places where you can work. How would a good farm job suit you?"

Jenny's heart sank. It was always the same. Everyone seemed to think she wanted to be a farm girl. She had helped at times on her Aunt May's farm, but never full-time.

"We've a nice spot at Dublands, just this side of Cockermouth." Miss Stalker's voice became less abrasive. "It would suit a young lass like you, but I'd expect you to work hard."

Jenny hesitated.

Miss Stalker continued: "Are you good at getting up in the morning? You are? Well that's summat. But can you make butter? You can't?" She thought for a moment. "What wages would you be expecting?"

Jenny was ready for that one. "Five pounds for the half-year."

"Five!" The woman's face stiffened. "That's more than I can afford. I pay £4."

Jenny did not flinch. "My friends get five."

"Do they now?" The woman pondered. "Money's very tight. How would £4 10 shillings suit you, and I learn you to make butter?"

Again Jenny hesitated. She knew that if she were not careful she might end up at the dreaded hirings.

"Well, if you changes your mind about a doctor's . . ." She began to turn away.

Jenny caught sight of Alice's worried expression. Without thinking she said: "I'll take it!"

It happened in a moment.

"Then that's all right," said Miss Stalker, returning quickly.

"You'll be wanting your yearls money." She opened a purse and pressed a shilling into Jenny's hand. The shilling token bound Jenny to be Miss Stalker's servant for the next six months.

"Now that's settled you call me Miss Stalker. Be outside here at three tomorrow. And don't be late, I don't approve of lateness."

The girls left. Alice linked an arm. "Heck, I didn't think you'd go with that 'un! She sounds a bit of a tart. But better than nowt, I suppose. Anyway let's find a café and I'll tell you about Jimmy, me boy friend! He digs graves at the cemetery, but really he wants to be a miner."

"He must like digging!" laughed Jenny.

"Aw, he's nice. Anyway, I bet lots of lads is chasing you, with your good looks!"

Jenny shook her head. "Not really."

"Oh ho, not really!"

"Well there is, sort of." There was Henry, well, no, there wasn't. Not that he had said anything. He never would.

4

A Bad Start

Dublands farm lay up a narrow forest track. It was evening as Miss Stalker and Jenny arrived by pony and trap and climbed down into a cobbled yard. Rain was falling and nothing could have seemed more miserable. Mud was everywhere. Apart from Miss Stalker, there appeared to be only one other person around, an old man who looked out from the barn across the yard.

They stepped into a slate-floor kitchen and Miss Stalker showed Jenny where she would sleep. "Make sure you keep your room tidy."

Jenny was shocked. Her room was not a room at all. It was a narrow den on the ground floor, half a passage blocked off with a board at one end and a curtain-less window with a dozen small panes down to floor level. She realised with dismay that anyone out in the yard could see straight in.

Miss Stalker handed her a candle. "Make this last. It'll cost a ha'penny from your wages if I have to get you another."

"Perhaps I'd better go to bed in the dark," suggested Jenny, annoyed. "That will save it burning away."

Miss Stalker glared. "Make sure it's out by nine o'clock!" she snapped.

"Now your jobs . . ."

The woman wasted no time in making sure Jenny knew her duties. She was to get up at six and light the kitchen stove.

"Once it's going, after breakfast I want the kitchen floor scrubbed on Wednesdays and Fridays, and don't be tramping on the floor till it's properly dry."

"I'll make sure it's dry," promised Jenny.

"On Mondays you get the clothes washed. I like sheets properly ironed and aired by Thursday so our beds can be changed. You can put clean sheets on both of them, but make yours last out: change yours once a fortnight."

It was clear the house had another occupant. Jenny wondered who it might be.

"We eat at 12.30 and in the afternoons there's the living room to turn out and the fire set. You'll need kindling for the next day."

The list of jobs went on.

They had a baked potato and a slice of bacon for supper. Afterwards Jenny cleared the dishes and washed up.

"Make sure you don't waste the candle," Miss Stalker reminded her.

The night was chilly and Jenny pulled her jersey over her nightdress and crept into bed. She had a feeling it was going to be difficult to please this woman.

Next morning matters started badly. Jenny broke a jug.

Miss Stalker hurried into the kitchen. "Brokken! What do you mean, brokken?"

"It fell off the dresser when the door slammed," Jenny explained.

"Oh did it! Well that's coming out of your wages, miss! Get it cleaned up, and finish the grate! I could have done the job twice over."

Jenny, annoyed with herself for being careless, rubbed the kitchen range until it shone. Miss Stalker appeared again, looking sour. "It'll do this time, but I've seen it look better."

Jenny smouldered angrily. Thank you, missis, for nothing, but she said it to herself. She became extra careful about everything she did. But it was hard work.

She was carrying a bucket of pigswill into the yard and was startled to see the old man in the barn doorway watching. He was rough looking with one side of his face badly wizened as if he had been burned. Realising she had seen him, he turned sharply back into the barn.

"I've told you," said Miss Stalker when Jenny mentioned it. "It's Jenks. He works for us. He's nothing to do with you."

Us? Who was us? There were a number of clues: she noticed a man's pipe on the mantelpiece; and later, when dusting the second bedroom, she realised the wardrobe was full of men's clothes. But they looked too good to be the hired man's.

Jenny was beginning to get her bearings. The farm clung to the side of a fell, a lime-washed building overlooking the head of Bassenthwaite Lake. Somewhere below lay the railway line to the little town of Cockermouth. At times between showers she could see smoke from a passing train. But the farm might have been in the middle of nowhere.

Later that day matters improved. Without warning, Miss Stalker's brother, Edgar, arrived home from a visit to Whitehaven. Jenny suddenly realised who *us* was, and all the men's clothes. She stopped sweeping, glad to rest.

Edgar was round-faced and whiskered. His curly hair was receding and he contrasted sharply with his sister's somewhat austere looks.

"So you're the new lass, are you?" he asked. "You'll 'appen not be a country lass?"

Jenny straightened her back. "I worked on my aunt's farm."

He smiled. "Is that so? Well I expect Annabel's got you sorted."

Mr Stalker's presence lightened the atmosphere at Dublands and Jenny went to bed that night feeling a lot happier. But already she was longing to see Aunt May again. Six months couldn't go fast enough.

5

To The Rescue

Henry and Snivel reached the end of a dark street. It was Carlisle at its gloomiest . . . a narrow jumble of shops and houses, wet cobblestones lit by the light from flickering gas lamps.

"Hey, listen!" said Henry.

Both could hear shouting.

"It's a bloke. He's being attacked!"

At the far end of the street two figures were struggling.

Henry turned his bike out into the middle.

"Sniv, come on!"

They set off towards the men. More shouts sounded and Henry pedalled hard, standing out of the saddle as he built up speed.

The attacker was lashing out with a stick. Henry homed his machine straight in – there was no time for anything else. He crashed headlong into the man.

"Yah! Yah! Yah!"

Snivel yelled wildly as Henry and the bike tumbled over onto the cobbles.

Their arrival changed everything. In a panic the thug dragged himself clear. Crab-like he scrambled across the ground, got to his feet and ran into the night.

A crumpled figure lay doubled up by a gas lamp, gasping for breath.

"My g-goodness. Thank you!"

He was an odd looking man in a red velveteen jacket and breeches.

"You all right, mister?"

They helped him to his feet.

"Yes – that is, no."

Henry saw blood coming from a deep gash in the man's right hand.

"I've fallen on something sharp."

He propped himself in a shop doorway. "Be all right in a minute."

But he was white-faced and his hand looked a mess.

"You must get that looked at mister. Tell you what . . ."

Henry dragged off his jersey. "Wrap this round, real tight."

"Goodness, no, not your jersey."

Henry knew what he was doing. The jersey was old and thin. He rolled it into a thick bandage and twisted it round the man's hand.

"You gotta keep it tight. It's what mum did when I cut me leg."

The man understood. It might help to slow the flow of blood.

"Thank you!" He grasped at the jersey. "You've come just in time!"

Now they could see the stranger more clearly they realised he was not exactly old, though his wing collar and the velveteen jacket gave him an odd theatrical appearance.

"I need to get to the Sands . . . to my caravan."

"I know the Sands!" exclaimed Henry. It was a big open market place in Carlisle centre where livestock was sold. He remembered it well. Nearly four years ago he and an Irish drover had driven 600 geese there after walking them across the wilds of northern Cumberland. "We'll go with you."

They walked slowly through the darkened streets pushing the bike and as they went they told the stranger how they had been travelling all day and had only just arrived.

The man's face lit in appreciation. "Lucky for me you did! And here we are."

The Sands surprised them. They had expected the place to be empty and dark, instead it was ablaze with flaring naphtha lamps. Hammering and voices sounded on all sides as men raced to put up lines of stalls and booths. The pungent smell of fizzling lamps filled the night.

"Tomorrow's Whit fair," explained the man. "Everyone's rushing to be ready. By the way, my name's Victor, Victor Biddall."

But the boys were only half listening. Warning shouts rang out. High up, a half-erected marquee began to tilt over. Standers-by raced to get clear but the danger was over quickly as two lines of men hauled on ropes and the marquee rose to its full height.

"Crikey!" marvelled Henry. The middle of the night and all this going on.

"This one's ours," said Victor Biddall. He stopped in front of a glittering green and gold coloured booth. It rose before them, amazingly ornate, carved with grotesque gnomes and ghoulish heads. Wooden steps went up to a pay box and a tunnel entrance to the inside.

Henry's heart beat excitedly. It was a travelling theatre! A board announced Biddall's Ghost Illusion, and along the top of the theatre in gold lettering a long line read: *Phantospectra Biddall's Ghost-O-dramas.*

"Ghosts?" Henry said, disbelievingly.

"Not real 'uns?" said Snivel.

Victor Biddall laughed. He had loosened his wing collar and was beginning to look less stressed. "Ah, ha! We Biddalls are famous for our ghosts."

The boys looked at him, but he seemed to be serious. "I don't believe in ghosts," said Henry.

"No one does," wheezed Snivel. "They're daft."

"Is that so! Well if you're here tomorrow I'll show you some ghosts that'll make you shiver with fright!"

Victor Biddall moved on down a line of caravans. Outside the biggest he pushed at a door. "Come on, come in."

At once there was a chorus of voices.

"He's here! Uncle Victor! What's happened? You're bleeding!"

6

Noisy Haven

The caravan was full of people sitting at a long table. A meal was being served.

"I'll tell you what's happened," declared Uncle Victor. "Rescued! That's what I've been. And these two brave lads are my rescuers!" Enthusiastically he explained how Henry and Snivel had sent the thug running.

The boys stood, embarrassed, and even more so as everyone broke into cheerful noisy applause.

"Bravo young 'uns! Come in! Come in! Sit down! But Victor, let's look at that hand."

Henry didn't know how they squeezed in, yet squeeze in they did. It was another world, hot and noisy, a snug caravan, bright with vases and shining ornaments, mahogany walls and panelling, a haven, at once warm and friendly.

"Let me introduce you," cried Uncle Victor.

And he did – too many for them to remember at one go – from the smallest boy to the grandest man of them all, the great showman himself, George Biddall, Victor's father.

Henry was hugely impressed.

George, grey haired, with a neatly trimmed beard and dressed in a smart jacket and leggings, listened courteously as he heard how the boys had charged at the attacker.

"Ran his bike straight into the beggar, head first," said Uncle Victor. "Bravest thing I've seen!"

"Well done!" said George. His voice was strong with an attractive nasal twang. His craggy face lit in approval. "A Biddall could not have done better! But you lads must be hungry! Selina, have we food for the boys?"

Mrs Biddall, deceptively small and delicate looking, waved a wooden spoon and signalled there was plenty to eat. She heaped steaming stew onto two plates and sent them along the table to Henry and Snivel.

"Eat up," she told them. "There's plenty more when that's done!"

How hungry they were! Starving! As they ate Henry explained how tomorrow was special because of the hirings; and how they would stand in the street with a straw in their mouths to signal they were for hire, and really it was just good luck they had turned up when Mr Victor was being attacked.

George was amused and impressed. "So you are farmer's boys are you?"

Henry thought carefully about that. "No, not exactly, it's just we stand more chance of getting a farm job than owt else. And we'll do all right. Lots get jobs at hirings."

"I used to chop firewood," said Snivel. "I could chop bags and bags of it in no time, just like that!"

"Then you'll be hired straight away!" said George, with a twinkle in his eye.

Such a time followed. A bald-headed man was introduced as Uncle Joey, a musician; he was another of George's sons. Joey rolled his eyes and rocked his head. "I'm a clown, really," he confided to Henry, and Henry could tell that he was. He picked up an accordion and soon the caravan filled with music. Beers were passed round. The boys supped half pints. Further along the table a beautiful slim-faced girl called Zella took hold of a large jug-sized tankard and to Henry's astonishment drank it down almost in one go. He guessed she was about fifteen.

As the dishes were cleared, songs followed, *D'Ye Ken John Peel?* and *I'll Take You Home Again, Kathleen*, and *Say, Watchman, What of the Night?* and many others until suddenly two o'clock began to chirp on a cuckoo clock and a giant yawn overcame Henry. Snivel, slumped alongside, was already dozing in a happy heap.

"Bedtime!" announced Selina. "We've a hard day come morning."

As the boys rose to go Uncle Victor said: "Where are you lads stopping?"

Henry blinked. In the excitement they had not yet been down to the den behind the pub.

"Not that it's far," he explained. "We'll easily get in."

Selina said: "There's no need! It's raining again. Why doesn't one of them doss down in Albert's bunk for tonight? And we can put a mattress on the floor for the other? There's room enough if you don't mind Joey snoring!"

"Who says I snore!" protested Joey.

The matter was settled.

"And if you give me your jersey," said Selina, "I'll see it's washed for you."

Stumbling with tiredness, they hurried through the wet and followed Uncle Victor along the line of caravans.

Henry, weary though he was, wanted to know something that had been bothering him. "Are you really an uncle?"

The showman hardly looked old enough.

Victor grinned. "Yes. And no! It's my show-name. The children use it, and we often get called uncle. Didn't you talk to old Mr Lodge? He's another."

Henry remembered an old man sitting at the far end of the table. Someone had said: "Meet Mr Lodge – Uncle Lodge. He's got the Aunt Sally and we look after him. But don't be upsetting him, he's a crack shot!"

"Was," the old man had said, his voice croaky. "Was a crack shot. Nowadays I miss sometimes!"

Whatever the case, he was another uncle.

They came to a small caravan, propped Henry's bike outside and climbed up four steps to a green carved door.

"You'll be all right in here," Victor told them. "Our other brother Albert is away in France for a day or two."

It was another snug den, with mahogany panels, bookshelves and cupboards. Two of the four bunks were empty, and the other two were stacked with boxes. Presiding over everything was a tall long-necked white pot cat sitting on a shelf above a stove.

They were too tired to take it all in properly. Henry handed Victor his jersey for Selina. He was the lucky one and got the spare bunk, and Uncle Victor spread a mattress and blanket on the floor for Snivel. The two lads settled down without thought of what the morning might bring. Later Joey arrived, stepped over Snivel and collapsed into the empty bunk. Soon he was snoring lustily, but Henry and Snivel heard nothing of him for their own snores were almost as loud.

7

Jenny in Charge

Up at Dublands, Miss Stalker carried a small suitcase out to the waiting pony and trap. Minutes later she added a second small case to the first. Jenny began to wonder if they were going to her sister Maud's for a whole week instead of just one night.

"Be sure you fasten both doors," she told Jenny. "And see the fireguard is round the grate. I don't want hot coals falling out!"

"Annabel," said Edgar, "Jenny will look after everything."

His sister pursed her lips. "I'm making sure that she does."

"I'm sure she will."

He smiled at Jenny.

"It's all right," said Jenny. She straightened her back so that she stood a shade taller. "I used to look after my Aunt May's place when she was away."

"She left you all alone?"

"Of course," said Jenny. "She trusts me."

Miss Stalker did not look any happier, but Jenny had decided that the woman was born to find fault no matter what.

They went out to the trap. Edgar said: "If you get any bother, Jenks will be around. Now we must be off."

The handyman was the only thing that made Jenny uneasy. She knew he had a key to the house but he rarely entered the kitchen, except to bring a can of milk from the byre. She had hardly spoken to him as he shambled about the farm.

She stood in the doorway as the trap disappeared and suddenly the place was quiet as if everything were listening. Well nothing would go wrong. She wouldn't let it.

She stoked the stove and did the worst job first and scrubbed the kitchen floor. Next she changed the bedding.

A bicycle bell in the yard came as a surprise. It was the postman and she hurried out.

"One for a Miss Atkinson."

"Why, that's me!"

A letter! Jenny had received only three letters in the whole of her life. She was very excited. It was from Aunt May.

She read it in the kitchen. The Liddles were now living in Silloth and were sadly missed. Bellow, her pony, was no longer limping, and had got over eating a barrow load of turnips, and was well again. Wicked Bellow!

The letter added: "Which brings me to mention, have you heard tell anything of Henry? His mother is very worried. She hasn't heard from him since he left for Carlisle."

Receiving a letter made Jenny more cheerful. She would write back and tell how she was in charge of the farm, and of course that she had not heard anything of Henry.

All day she kept herself busy. At dusk she lit a paraffin lamp and fastened the back door, turning the key in the lock until it clicked loudly. The front door was different. The lock was broken but it had a large bolt and she slid it firmly into place. Nothing would force that in a hurry. She wasn't feeling nervous, really, but she knew she must do the job properly and she carried the lamp from room to room to make sure all the windows were secure. Her own window had lost its catch and someone had knocked a nail in to jam it. She peered out into the yard but nothing seemed unusual.

She was glad to get back to the friendly warmth of the kitchen where she heated up a bowl of stew. The fire was burning well and because she was in charge she sat in Miss Stalker's rocking chair and read the letter again. Despite herself she found she was wondering where Henry was.

Nine o'clock was striking before she went to bed. Seeing the old copper bedpan hanging up with its long wooden handle gave her an idea. Tonight she would enjoy a warm bed herself. Daringly she took Mrs Stalker's stone hot water bottle from a cupboard and filled it from the kettle. She put on her nightdress, wrapped a towel round the bottle and soon lay under the covers with her feet propped against its comforting heat. Happily warm, she fell asleep.

8
Shots In The Night

A faint sound roused her. For several moments Jenny lay in bed not quite asleep, not quite awake. She gave a shiver. It was as if something had moved past her in the bedroom gloom. What had woken her?

But nothing was there. Subdued moonlight lit the tall window, its panes blank with condensation. She must have been dreaming.

A moment later she sat up sharply. A scraping noise sounded on the glass. It came again, a long rasping. Her heart pounding, she got out of bed and listened. She could make out a faint shadow outside.

At the same instant a gust of air hit her as a pane of glass was removed. Jenny waited no longer. Grabbing the bedpan off the wall, she turned it round, rested it on the glass for a moment then thrust the pole out through the gap as hard as she could.

"Aaaaaah!"

A cry of pain filled the night. Not waiting, she rammed the handle out again. Again it struck something hard, and then she almost collapsed with fright as a pane of glass was smashed to pieces.

Jenks! She needed help. Dropping the bedpan, she raced to the back door. Risking everything, she turned the key and ran barefooted across the cobbles and knocked furiously on the barn door.

"Jenks! Jenks! There's a burglar!"

A dog started barking furiously.

Inside, Jenks sat slumped, his face down on the table. He looked up as she entered. "Whatsamarra?"

Jenny groaned. He had been drinking!

Even so, as she gasped out again about an intruder he got to his feet.

"B-brokken a winda, ya say? Quiet, Shep, quiet!"

They crossed the yard with a lantern and Jenny showed him the window. "His hand was right inside!"

Glass fragments lay scattered on the frosty ground.

"Got him in the face, did ya?"

Jenny was shivering and hopping about on her frozen feet, wishing she had a blanket. "I don't know! I just did it."

Jenks was sobering up quickly enough now. "A prowler, that's what. Get yourself inside in the warm; I'll teach the beggar what's what."

In the kitchen Jenks reached a shotgun down from a beam and pulled open a drawer. He loaded it with cartridges.

"Stay where ya are missy while I see round the yard."

Several tense minutes passed, then Jenny was startled by a loud bang as the gun was fired. Seconds later a second shot sounded.

When the door opened Jenny was shaking.

"What's happened? You've not shot someone have you?"

He laughed at her expression.

"Nay. I shot in the air. But I reckon I've given him a bit of a fright!"

"Me too!"

Still trembling, Jenny brewed a pot of tea and raided the cake tin. Then they sat by the remains of the fire and she told again how she had pushed the panhandle through the gap.

"Given him summat to think about, ya have!" He raked up the coals. "He must 'ave seen the master and the missis leaving and thought the place empty. Now I'll tell ya what, you keep the doors locked, and I'll keep an eye on the yard. He'll not come back."

Jenny smiled gratefully. At the same time she sensed that something was bothering him.

"Is everything all right?"

"Aye, well . . . that is, I wouldn't be wanting them to know – not Miss Stalker, that is, how I'd had a drop to drink, like."

"Oh, no. I won't say a thing!"

He nodded pensively. He was sober enough now. "That would be real kind of you, missy. Me not having another job to hand."

"Not a word," promised Jenny. "I'd never have managed without you!"

Jenks left and Jenny locked up. She refilled the hot water bottle and got back into bed. What a tale she would tell Aunt May!

The Stalkers arrived home the next evening. The news about an intruder turned Annabel's face white. All four went out to examine the window. During the day Jenny had filled the gaps with cardboard to keep out the draught.

Annabel was grim faced. "I told you we shouldn't have left her in charge. You never listen."

"Now, Annabel, don't start that! It's not Jenny's fault. The lass has had a bit of a fright. Some beggar's tried to get in. She's saved us a lot of trouble."

Jenny said: "You should thank Jenks as well. It would have been a lot worse without his help."

The old man gave her a grateful smile.

"Whoever it was, you got him?"

"With the bedpan . . . the handle," Jenny explained. "But all I did was push it out through the window."

"You've done well," Edgar told Jenny.

Back indoors, Miss Stalker examined the bedpan. The wooden handle was scratched.

"I'll tell you this," she told Edgar severely. "It's going to be a long time before we go away again."

She was going to be proved wrong.

9

Two For Hire

A noisy crowd filled the street. The sky was still grey and overcast but at least it had stopped raining. Henry, engulfed in one of Joey's shirts, pushed with Snivel into the middle of the crush and tried to look as if going to Carlisle hirings was something they did every day. But he was not looking forward to it. A lot depended on the next couple of hours.

"They all look like farmers."

"H-how'd ya know?"

"I just do," said Henry. He could recognise a farmer anywhere. "We've gotta get a good 'un."

Both put short pieces of straw between their lips. Everyone did it, to show they wanted to find work.

"Don't go chewing it," warned Henry, "or it won't last!"

Snivel did as told, but it was hard not to chew at a bit of straw when it was sticking out of your mouth.

They had been up since six when Selina had given them bread and jam and mugs of tea. By seven the entire Ghost Show team was hurrying out to prepare the theatre for the first performance. Henry was envious. Everyone seemed to know what to do. A gang of Biddalls children raced off with a wheeled barrel to fill it with water, a big silent man called Rudge went to the riverside to feed the horses, others were repainting chipped woodwork at the front of the theatre which the lads now saw was two caravans put end to end. Henry tried to imagine what it was like, travelling from fair to fair. It was an exciting thought.

Uncle Victor paused. "Leave your bike; we'll keep an eye on it, and make sure you come and see us after you've got jobs. I'll show you some real ghosts!"

They grinned, but there was no time for talk.

"Right!" called George. "Let's get the theatre open. Can we get the music sorted?"

Joey and another clown staggered up the steps carrying a glittering black and gold harmonium. Henry could hardly take his eyes off it, but it was time to be going.

They stood in the middle of the crowd.

"Just leave this to me," said Snivel. "I'll get us jobs as quick as owt."

"Oh?" said Henry, surprised.

Snivel smirked and squared his little shoulders. "Just watch us; you'll see."

A fat unshaven man halted. "Are you for hire?" he demanded of Henry. Everything about him was hairy, the backs of his hands, his chins, his unkempt head.

"Aye, master."

"And what can you do, then?"

Henry knew he had to sound confident, but before he could answer Snivel stepped forward, his thumbs hooked importantly onto each side of his jersey.

Little though he was, he spoke loudly. "You've come to the right place, mister. Me and me pal can do owt."

"Nay!" The man cut in impatiently. "I isn't wanting to hire two on you."

Snivel wasn't put off. "But we is real good workers mister, we can . . ."

The man was already walking away.

"Don't worry," Snivel told Henry hurriedly. "Just a try-out."

But Henry was worried. It wasn't going to be easy to find someone who'd take both of them. Snivel's small build would probably put people off.

A lean-faced man paused. "For hire, are ya? And what can ya do?"

"We can do owt," said Snivel. "Dig ditches, spread muck, milk cows, there's nowt we can't do."

"Aye? You can milk can ya?" The man eyed Snivel's grubby hands.

"I'm quick at it," bragged Snivel. He stood, both feet spread firmly on the ground, looking confident. "Done it all me life."

The man's eyes narrowed. "Quick are ya? As it happens I could use a good milker. How quick are you with a cow, a big 'un say with six teats?"

Henry's mouth opened in alarm.

"Six, eight, ten!" declared Snivel boldly. "Nowt to it! Just pull 'em and squeeze!"

"Ten?" said the farmer. "Five in each hand, eh!"

The man left, rumbling with laughter.

Henry boiled over. "You gormless twit! Cows haven't got ten teats!"

"Course they have!" blustered Snivel. "I've seen 'em."

"You're lying! Just shut up. From now on I'll do the talking."

"Nay . . ."

"Shut up!" snapped Henry. "And quit bragging."

The day wore on. Farmers and their wives kept stopping to question them. But no one wanted to hire the two of them together.

Eventually Snivel said: "If ya ask me this is right stupid."

"Stupid?" said Henry, annoyed. "D'ya want a job or don't ya? If we get nowt here we'll have to try at Penrith next week."

As one o'clock struck, scarcely a dozen farm hands were left standing around talking. Carlisle hirings were over.

"I told ya it was no good," said Snivel, scowling. "What we gonna do?"

Henry was downcast. "I dunno."

He had no real plan. They walked away. "We'll look round the town a day or two. We'll find summat."

But getting a job wasn't Snivel's only trouble.

"It's all right for you . . ."

He trailed off.

Henry glared. "What?"

Snivel said nothing.

"What?" demanded Henry.

"I ain't got no money."

That was a new one! "Didn't the wood yard pay you?"

Snivel didn't answer.

"They must have! Empty ya pockets."

Snivel didn't move.

"Do it!"

Henry grabbed at Snivel's jersey.

Something shiny fell onto the cobbles.

"Where'd ya get that?" demanded Henry. "That's the roadman's knife."

"I found it," said Snivel.

He snatched it back.

"You didn't! You've pinched it."

"I didn't. It was on the grass."

"Give it here!"

But Snivel made no move to return it.

Henry felt a swell of anger. He grabbed Snivel. A moment later they were punching one another.

"It was on the grass, I told ya!"

Henry wrestled Snivel to the ground.

"Ouch! Gerroff! You're a bully."

"And you're a thief! A rotten thief. That was Charlie's knife."

Snivel seized Henry's head and grabbed at an ear.

Henry let out a yell, pummelling Snivel in the ribs.

"That'll teach you, you lousy titch!"

They tumbled to the cobbles, punching madly. But the struggle proved too much for Snivel. Exhausted, he flopped back and quite suddenly he screwed up, and began coughing loudly.

"Hey," said Henry, surprised. Snivel was looking ill. "You all right?"

"It's me chest," Snivel gasped. "I's got me dad's w-wheezes."

Henry hesitated, then he put out a hand and pulled him up off the cobbles.

Snivel went on coughing. "G-give us a minute. It'll go."

They stood a while and gradually Snivel's breathing eased. He felt in a pocket. Sheepishly he handed Henry the knife. "It *was* on the grass. But I shouldn't have taken it. I thought it would come in handy."

"Yeah, but you gotta stop pinching stuff! I don't want to be around when you get caught."

"Hey, ya ain't leaving us is ya?"

An anxious note had crept in.

Henry stood, uncertain.

Snivel's white face decided him.

"We'll stick together for now."

"I was just borrowing the knife."

"Aye, all right."

Suddenly Henry grinned. "Tell you what, you've got a whopping black eye coming!"

"Thanks." Snivel smirked, wincing with the effort. "Wait till you see your nose."

"You'd make a proper good boxer, you would," said Henry appreciatively. "You've a good right-hander."

"Have I?"

"For a titch."

"What we gonna do for money?"

Henry felt at his jacket pocket. He had four shillings tied up in a piece of rag. Snivel knew nothing about them, but now they'd have to use them. "We can last a few days, I'll buy us grub, but you gotta pay me back when you get a job."

Snivel looked surprised. "Pay ya? I mean, yeah, course."

Henry glanced across the empty square. Snivel was a bit of a twerp but he wasn't all that bad. Sooner or later they would get jobs. All Henry wanted right now was to get away from the place. It was becoming depressing. "Let's go and see them ghosts."

"Yeah!" Snivel's face brightened. "Do ya think they're real uns?"

"Course not!"

Henry didn't believe in ghosts. All the same, they were in for a surprise, if not exactly a fright.

10

Ghostly Goings On

Rousing organ music and an exciting tattoo of beating drums set the lads racing across to the Sands. Gloomy though the day, they arrived to find the showground crowded. Such a din! Yells and shrieks, swirling merry-go-rounds, a wild surging swoosh of the swingboats.

They reached the Ghost Show as an ear-splitting crash of cymbals sounded. A clown stepped onto the stage fronting the booth waving a giant megaphone. The man's voice boomed out.

"La-dies and gennelmen! Step up! Step up! Biddall's Ghosts! The show is about to begin!"

Henry almost failed to recognise Joey. The clown wore a bright orange and yellow costume. His nose was big and red and shiny. But it was his huge wooden-soled shoes that made the crowd gasp, more than two-foot long, giant black clompers, he rose up now, standing on the toes, balancing marvellously.

"Don't hang back gennelmen!" he bellowed. "Step inside, bring the wife and give her a fright!"

He swayed alarmingly and Henry gasped. Surely he was going to fall! But no! Upright again.

"Only tuppence, ladies and gennelmen! Children just one penny!"

Lads in the crowd jeered. Tough young lads, farm lads. Leary whistles sounded as a girl danced across the entrance stage. More jeers as a chalk-faced man crept after her, then startled cries as a gush of fire poured from his mouth.

"Wow! C'mon," gasped Henry.

Excited, he tugged Snivel onto the steps up to the pay box.

"Bravo, lads! You've come!" A scary green face grinned at them from behind the glass. It was Uncle Victor, streaked in paint. "So who's been in a fight? – that's a lovely black eye!"

The boys looked sheepish

"Never mind, in you go. No need to pay! Not after the way you helped us."

He waved his bandaged hand.

The boys entered a dark entrance tunnel. Three steps and suddenly:

Yaaaaah!

A shriek and an explosive rattle. A strange white apparition tumbled straight at them. A skeleton, only to vanish – zap!

"Ow! Help!"

They had ducked, but nothing was there.

"Blimey! Where's it gone?"

There was no chance of finding out. People were surging in behind them, wanting seats.

The theatre was dark and hot. Sputtering acetylene lamps hissed, filling the place with a pungent gassy smell.

The lads had hardly time to squash onto a bench.

Barooooooom!

41

The crash of harmonium music filled the theatre, then somehow it turned itself into *God Save the Queen*. As it died away eighty people fell silent. Two musicians started to play a banjo and bones medley, nothing strange, nothing . . .

A gasp rippled through the audience. A ghostly cowled figure was rising up behind the banjo player. Unseen by either of the musicians, it loomed, its bony skull staring out of black eyeless sockets.

People at the front shrank back nervously, then they almost tumbled off the benches in fright as the ghost seemed to strike at the man, knocking him down. His chilling cry was still echoing as the phantom vanished.

A moment later the ghostly figure was rising behind the man who was playing the bones. Young girls, at the back of the theatre, suddenly too frightened to watch, hid their faces behind their hands.

The ghost lunged at the man and his shriek filled the place. The two musicians turned accusingly on one another. They punched and kicked, rolling across the boards as the ghost faded.

Henry's face turned cold. It couldn't be a ghost! He knew it couldn't. But it was scary.

A mother in a shawl appeared on the stage and sat beside a cradle, guarding her dying child.

Snivel, his face drawn and white, pointed up. "Look!"

High above, a shimmering angel with shining wings flew slowly into sight, a flickering light encompassing her.

Everyone could see that the angel's wings did not move, yet she was flying! The audience stared open mouthed as she floated across the stage.

Henry was baffled. There were no wires. How could she fly?

Dramatically the child died amid a wail of music. The angel paused, before she began to drift away carrying the child with her.

Only at the last moment did the shimmering creature sense danger. Warning yells sounded. Already the audience had seen the ghoulish figure rising behind her, its mouth open, menacing, fanged. Everyone gasped. Everyone saw it happen. The angel vanished. The ghoul had swallowed her.

Baroooooooom! Baroooooooom! Baroooooooom!

Hearts leapt. The music rose in a noisy wave then dramatically died away until there was only a single eerie note, low, haunting, scaring. Suddenly the stage was empty.

Henry was at a loss.

"How've they done that?"

No one round them knew. It was easy now to see that there were no wires, yet the angel clearly had flown. People were arguing. No one believed in ghosts . . . it was mirrors. It must be.

But the show wasn't over! A jumble of bones began to crawl across the boards. One by one the bones started to join up until abruptly they heaved upright into a skeleton and pointed a bony hand at the crowd.

Uneasy laughter sounded, yet with it was mixed a certain sense of awe.

Then it was over. The skeleton vanished into the dark. The music died away.

"That angel really flew!" said Henry, baffled.

"Nay. There was wires," asserted Snivel. He was positive. "I could see 'em. Lots of 'em."

"You didn't! There wasn't any. And the ghosts didn't have any."

"Well they must have," insisted Snivel, determined to be right.

Henry could no more be sure how it was done than anyone else. But he knew Snivel was wrong. In any case there had been something strangely familiar about the angel.

"I've seen her before. She was at the table."

"Your girl friend is she!"

"Don't be daft! Of course she isn't."

The afternoon was fading. They were nearly the last to leave.

"Hello, lads! Hello!"

Uncle Victor came out. "How was it?"

Their excited faces told him everything.

"Smashing! Real weird."

"Yeah," said Snivel.

"But how do you do it?"

"Ah-ha!" The man gave a crafty smile. "I don't suppose you want to see it again?"

They did. And would have stayed for a third time but the second performance did not end well. As the last ghoulish figure faded, the harmonium music began to roll towards a grand climax . . . but it never got there.

The harmonium began to fade away and the theatre became silent. Perhaps the audience thought it was part of the show, but Henry realised that something was wrong.

11

Letter From Jenny

Dear Aunt May,

I was so happy to get your lovely letter and pleased to know how well you are and to tell you I am well as well and everything is really all right.

Well I got a job in this little farm called Dublands way up on the fell-side. There's a beautiful view across the lake to Skiddaw and one day cousin Alice and me plan to climb right up to the top of it together because the sight is supposed to be one of the best in all of Cumberland and I can believe it is because it looks so high.

I didn't get a doctor's place. There are just four of us here at this farm. Miss Stalker and her brother, Mr Stalker, and a hired man who drinks a lot, and me. Mr Stalker is very kind even if his sister is starchy. She is always saying things are not properly done but I saw her button boots when she was polishing them and they were hardly shiny when she had finished them, so she needn't talk!

You said about Henry, I don't know anything about him anymore. So he was going to Carlisle? He's likely on some farm and too tired to write but it's just like a lad not to. If I hear anything I'll tell you but I don't suppose I will because of course I am here for six months and no chance of getting out or going anywhere.

One thing is certain, I promise I will come and see you when the six months is over. I'm not going to stay here forever.

From your loving niece, Jenny.

12

Emergency Repairs

People were standing round the harmonium looking worried. They had opened up the hinged lid and were peering inside, worried because time was going and because the first evening show was due to start.

Victor was dejected; his injured hand still bandaged just when he was most needed. "Some of the reeds could be blocked. We need our Albert!"

Victor and his brother Albert between them ensured the harmonium was always working, but Albert was still away in France.

Henry moved closer so that he could listen. The ornately painted harmonium had a music rack, which opened into an ornamental scroll with two cut-out figures holding flutes or pipes. He longed to help.

George arrived. The showman did not hesitate. "Joey, get out the piano accordion."

Groans sounded.

Victor said "The old organ's getting past it."

"Yes, but we can't manage without it," said George.

Without creepy music the ghosts were not as frightening.

Henry bit at his lip. The harmonium was none of his business but he was itching to take a look inside at the works.

He glanced at the beautiful Zella and caught her eye. She was frowning and without knowing exactly why he suddenly wanted to impress her.

Despite his nervousness, he determined to risk it. "Could I have a look?" he asked George. "I mean, just for a moment? I mean, I fix things at home."

George smiled: "Thank you, lad. I'm sorry, but we'll have to get a professional repair man."

Henry nodded, but he did not give up.

"He's really good at fixing things," said Snivel. "I've seen him fix hundreds of things."

"Just a quick look," said Henry. Before anyone could stop him he moved in close and peered down inside at the long line of keys.

"Hey. What's he doing?"

The showman hesitated, then said: "Let him look."

It wasn't easy to see, but Henry detected a speck of white between two of the keys.

"There's a bit of summat down on that side."

George lent over but he could see nothing out of the ordinary.

"I might be able to get at it," said Henry, "if you don't mind us trying? I think I can reach it."

George had observed Henry's hands, small and slim like Victor's. And the lad had the added benefit of young sight.

"All right, have a go."

It was the smallest of fragments, like the end of a bit of thread. Henry tried to catch it between his thumb and fingernails. He was feeling excited and it didn't help. Twice he failed to get a hold, but the third time he managed to nip it. Holding his breath, he pulled out a cotton-like thread and held it up.

"Well," said George, "however did that get in there?" It was a piece of dried grass.

At the same time, George knew that this alone would not have caused the harmonium to go wrong.

Henry guessed that, too. Without asking, he undid hooks at each end of the keyboard and tilted it up.

He reached in and felt carefully along the keys but not until he reached the far end did he find the cause of trouble. He lifted out a ragged clump of shredded papers and feathers.

There were exclamations of surprise.

"What is it?"

"Well I'm blowed," said George. "It's a mouse's nest. No wonder we've been getting some funny noises!"

Henry grinned as everyone examined the nest. There was even a chewed nutshell among the scraps.

Joey peered in. "The blooming thing's gnawed at the black keys, too!"

George lowered everything back into place.

"Will it work now?" said Victor.

"Let's find out," said George.

He sat on the seat, put his feet on the carpeted pedals and began to pump at the bellows. They hissed as he waited until there was enough pressure before he tried the keys.

The theatre filled with a swirl of exciting notes.

"Hurrah! Now how's that!"

Gleeful grins filled the place. George turned to Henry, nodded sagely and swung into *For He's A Jolly Good Fellow.*

"Good lad," he told Henry enthusiastically. "Well done. Couldn't be better!"

For the second time in two days the Biddalls broke into spontaneous applause. Even Zella's beautiful face shone with an engaging smile of approval so that Henry almost blushed.

But no time to linger. "Enough!" George waved a hand. "I want everything ready in ten minutes!"

Pandemonium! They raced to clear up. Everything was going to be all right.

The evening show was in full swing. Eight o'clock, nine o'clock, ten . . . the night shone with hissing naphtha lamps. Like a magical giant engine, the Sands Fair glittered and heaved as spectators swamped the ground. Shouts and laughter. Ghostly shrieks, booming music, and wild yells, especially from the boxing booth as farm lads took on the boxers, a £3 prize if they lasted four rounds. (None ever did).

Old Mr Lodge saw the lads and waved. "Hello, hello! Come and have a free go on my Aunt Sally."

His stall stood alongside the Ghost Show lit by a line of lamps. Late though it was, it was alive with hefty thunks as people tried their luck and threw balls, whacking the battered targets – a wooden line of womens' heads in bonnets, all chewing at clay pipes.

"You lads have done a good job," exclaimed the old man. "You fixed it just in time!"

Henry's face shone. "It wasn't that much wrong."

Snivel chimed in: "Mrs Biddall says we can stop a second night."

"Has she now? Well that's good. Here . . ."

Mr Lodge handed them some balls. "Try your luck."

"But what if we win?" said Henry.

"Then you get a prize," said Mr Lodge.

All three of Henry's throws hit the targets but good shot though he was he failed to knock anything over. He gave Snivel a quick grin; it was harder than it looked.

Snivel took aim and immediately knocked a head off its post.

"Well done!" exclaimed Mr Lodge.

Snivel, pleased with himself, had two more goes. To the old man's surprise a second head went flying.

"Goodness. That's good throwing! That deserves a special prize."

He reached for a big tin and handed it to Snivel. "No, no, take it. You hit the target good and proper."

It was a tin of Royal Blue toffee.

"So you're farm lads, are you?"

"Well, not exactly," said Henry. "We can do lots of things. I want to travel and see lots of places!"

"Me, too," said Snivel.

The old man looked amused.

"Oh yes, do you? And where might that be?"

"Everywhere."

They left, and Snivel opened the Royal Blues and shared them with Henry.

The last ghostly phantom vanished soon after half past eleven. The boys, more tired than they had ever been, sighed with relief.

Soon it would be Sunday. Selina had told Henry that George always observed the Sabbath so there would be no more ghosts now until they opened in Cockermouth on Monday.

But to the boys' surprise, middle of the night though it was, work was not over. First there were welcome refreshments.

Two figures appeared, Selina and Zella, carrying trays loaded with tea and hefty beef sandwiches. For ten welcome minutes everyone took a break, standing around eating and drinking.

Zella handed Henry a steaming mug. He felt a wave of shyness, but her earlier approving smile had been encouraging. She was truly beautiful. Her mood, though, had changed as he discovered.

"You're the angel, aren't you?" he said. "What flies about."

"Oh, and who says?"

Her nose was pert, and turned up.

"I saw you. I know it was you."

"Did you! Well lots see me."

"But you are real good. Proper creepy."

She smirked. "You're just another bumpkin, like the rest, aren't you?"

Henry felt himself going red.

"No I isn't: I'm from Silloth."

"Same thing."

"It isn't! I went and fixed the harmonium!"

She pulled a pouty face and turned away. Henry frowned. Girls! He'd keep his mouth shut next time.

"Right," called George. "Let's start! Come morning, I want us on the road good and early."

It was beginning to rain again but no one paused. Dark though it was, the Biddalls' men and women began to dismantle the theatre. Everyone worked quickly.

Henry and Snivel, not sure what to do, stood around.

Uncle Victor appeared. How tired were they? Not at all! Well, would they mind carrying the precious gilded gnome heads to Joey? They helped at once. Slung underneath each caravan were belly boxes, big empty storage spaces. Joey began packing the heads away. One box, however, was kept empty.

"We might be needing that," he told Henry. "And by the way, George wants to see you in the morning."

"Me? What for?"

But the clown turned away. Even if he knew, he wasn't saying.

All night long it rained. Henry woke once as it pounded the caravan roof and realised he'd been dreaming about Zella. She was a real snooty, but oh so beautiful. He was still thinking this as he fell asleep again.

13

Show Lads

Henry climbed up into George and Selina's caravan. The Ghost Show would be leaving soon. It had just gone nine in the morning and hardly light, the sky the colour of lead. Rain had fallen most of the night but now at last it had stopped.

"Come in, Henry." Selina reached for the teapot. "You're just in time for a cuppa."

George closed the lid of the black cashbox.

"Sit down, Henry, sit down."

The showman rubbed his beard and eyed the boy. Sixteen was he, nearly seventeen? Not exactly strong looking but certainly resourceful.

"I see you are good at mechanical things."

Henry's face lit up. "Nay, it was nowt."

Handy Henry. Elizabeth, his mother, used to call him that.

"Well you know we are very grateful you fixed the harmonium."

The showman pushed the sugar jar across. "As it is, I hear you didn't have much luck at the hirings."

Henry couldn't disguise his feelings. The hirings had been a disaster. "We're going to try down at Penrith. Folk says there's good hirings at Penrith."

"Yes, so I have heard." George sat back in his seat. "Well, we're not going to Penrith this trip; as you know we're off in the next couple of hours to Cockermouth. It's their hirings tomorrow. But I've been wondering – how would you like to join the Ghost Show as a helper, in case the harmonium dies on us again? Just for the week, that is. Of course, there'd be other jobs, as well."

Henry's senses began to race.

George added more sugar to his own tea. "Victor's injured hand is causing him a bit of trouble, to do any repairs anyway, and Albert's not back. We could certainly use the help."

Henry caught Selina's smile of encouragement.

A Ghost Show job!

"Crikey! I'd be right pleased."

But there was a problem.

"You'd be paid, of course," said George. "Not a fortune because money's tight. There'll be plenty to do, selling gingerbread, keeping the theatre clean, fetching and carrying – but I must warn you it could make it hard for you to get farm work later on. You'll have missed several of the main hirings for another six months."

Henry ignored the thought of hirings. The hirings were not the problem, at least not yet. "It's Snivel," he explained. "He's my pal."

George's face became grave. "Oh, I see. Well, I wasn't thinking of taking on two of you." He glanced across to Selina. She seemed uneasy.

"I don't think we can manage to take him on just now."

"But he doesn't eat much," said Henry. "At least, not a lot."

The showman laughed out loud. "Doesn't he! Well that's handy to know."

"He could share my wages," offered Henry.

"No, no." George scratched at his beard and thought for a moment. "That wouldn't be necessary." He paused to reflect. "All right – the two of you can come, for a week. But he'll have to work hard. You both will. It's nearly all one-night stands. A constant putting up the show and taking it down again. We don't have a starting time; in fact we don't have a finishing time either. If business is good it'll be twenty or more shows a day, and getting on for a midnight finish often enough. I'll not disguise that it's hard going."

Henry grinned with relief. "Snivel won't mind that. He's never been anywhere, not properly. Not on a real adventure."

"Is that so?" The showman's eyebrows rose. "Then it is certainly time he did!"

Selina smiled and refilled their cups. "If you don't mind my asking, Henry, what's your full name?"

"Hodgekin – Henry Hodgekin."

"Oh, yes. It's a good name." She glanced at George. "And your little friend Snivel, have you known him long?"

"No, but he's all right," affirmed Henry. "Once he gets going."

Selina seemed satisfied. Snivel had struck her as a bit shifty, but if Henry vouched for him then that was all right. As it was, Henry was obviously an enterprising lad.

There was someone at the door. It was Uncle Victor. He came inside looking worried.

George said: "We've just been mentioning your name."

Victor gave a wry smile. "It's bad news. I've just heard, the road out of town is flooded!"

George put down his cup. "Confound it! Whereabouts?"

"A place called Caldewgate."

George knew the spot. He had taken that road before.

"They say the horses won't be able to get through," said Victor.

George stood up and went outside to look up. The sky was an endless grey, full of clouds racing across the rooftops.

"Really bad?"

"The fire brigade's trying to pump it away into the river. They reckon it'll take hours."

George buttoned his jacket. They had to get to Cockermouth by tomorrow morning.

"Right! Let's take a look."

Henry joined George and Victor and walked through the town centre. At Caldewgate, water was pouring across the road. It looked bad. People were watching from upstairs windows in nearby houses as firemen worked a large hand-pump.

Henry eyed the torrent. How deep was it? Risking it, he tried stepping in, but quickly pulled back. It was deceptive; the water tugged at his legs and in a moment swirled above his knees.

"Take care!" warned George. "There's a bit of a current. As it is, Victor, get someone down here to keep watch. Get Kyle. And tell everyone to get harnessed up. We might have a long wait, but I want everything ready to start the moment it's gone down far enough."

14

Two New Hands

Henry found Snivel and told him the news. The titch looked smug. "Yeah, I knew all along as they'd give us jobs," he bragged.

"You what?"

"I telled ya." He hooked his thumbs into the edges of his jersey. "I knew all along!"

"Don't talk daft," said Henry. "You weren't even going to get a job till I said. You didn't know owt."

"Course I did!"

"Hah! You're bats. Anyway, George wants us to go and see Rudge. Everyone's gotta be ready the moment the water goes down."

Henry was annoyed. His boots were still squelching as he set off for the river. Fed up with the titch, he shoved Snivel on ahead keeping him going.

"Hey, watch it!"

"Just keep moving," ordered Henry.

Blooming smug pants!

Rudge was getting ready to brush the horses. He was a tough looking muscular man with a quiet manner. A cluster of powerful Clydesdale greys stood near him under a makeshift canvas shelter.

"So you're starting work with us, are you?"

"How do you know that?" said Henry, astonished. It seemed no time since he had left George.

Rudge's face never changed, never smiled, though both lads sensed that he was kind enough. "No secrets here, lads. Seems we're going to be stuck here an hour or two by the sound of things, and there's plenty to do. Have you brushed a hoss down? No? Then now's your chance to learn summat useful."

Rudge moved in among the horses, slapping their flanks. They were tethered on a line under the shelter.

"This is Nelson – he's the boss hoss – and this is Skipper, and these is Bob-Boy and Jasper – he's a bit bad tempered is Jasper, and there's Diamond, and Billy, and Tinker . . ."

Nelson stamped heavily at the ground. Henry, who had rarely had anything to do with horses, could tell he was special. He looked so solid and strong.

Several other showmen were already busy getting the horses ready. A cautious Henry and a nervous Snivel guided by Rudge prepared to help brush Nelson's silky flanks.

"Before you start, talk to him a bit. Get him used to you. And place your free hand flat on him while you work. It helps keep him calm. And don't be scared. Just remember he enjoys it."

It took a lot of brushing before Rudge decided that Nelson was well groomed. Then they turned to Skipper. The two, Nelson and Skipper, would pull George's van.

The lads were slower at brushing than Rudge but he said nothing and gradually even Snivel lost his nervousness. And it was true; the horses did seem to enjoy the strokes of the brushes.

Several paused to look at the new hands, passing mildly sarcastic remarks. Old Mr Lodge nodded his approval. Even Zella stopped to watch.

At last they finished. Snivel said wryly: "Got yourself two girls now, 'aven't ya!"

"What? Don't be daft."

Snivel smirked knowingly.

"Fancies you she does. I seen her looking."

"Who'd you mean?"

"You know who – that Zella"

"Says who? She don't even like me."

"Bet she does. She's a good looker, but she don't half know it."

"So?"

"So they're hard as brass is them pretty uns. That's what me dad says. Right tough."

Henry grinned. "She knows how to scowl when she wants."

In fact Henry had noticed Zella's glances.

The afternoon sped by and everyone broke off for sandwiches and mugs of tea. The canvas shelters had been dismantled. The horses and the theatre wagons waited. Everything was ready for the road.

But the floodwater was taking a long time to subside. Watch was kept all evening and not until eleven o'clock was striking did a cluster of men and women gather yet again with their lanterns at the water's edge.

George held up his lantern.

The flood had gone down dramatically. The water was little more than inches deep.

"It's safe enough. Pass the word along. Ten minutes, everyone, then let's be away."

15

Snivel Is Frightened

The caravans prepared to move off. The night filled with the sound of people calling, doors slamming and the clatter of horses' hooves.

Henry and Snivel were bleary eyed. Selina said: "We've changed your sleeping arrangements a bit. Rudge, show them, will you?"

Rudge led them to the end van.

"You'll have to swap places each time you take a kip," the horseman explained. "But it'll stop Joey having to step over you."

This time Snivel was the lucky one and got the spare bunk. Henry found out now why one of the belly boxes had been kept empty.

"Wedge it open with this stick," advised the horseman.

Henry ducked under the van. Some of the boxes opened sideways but this one had a lid. He climbed in with his pack and found there was a blanket. If he didn't try to stretch out too much he had just enough room.

Rudge lowered the lid.

Henry quickly propped it higher.

"You all right?"

The lantern gleamed through a six-inch gap.

"Aye, course. But how did you know we was working for you?" Rudge's eyes shone brightly. "Ah. A family meeting. The Biddalls, we allus talk things over fust."

"But you didn't know about Snivel."

"We guessed," said the horseman. "It wasn't difficult."

They were off. Shouts and the clatter of iron-rimmed wheels filled the night. The two strongest greys, Nelson and Skipper, led the way along the town streets, hauling the first of the theatre vans, and soon a line of others followed in behind, candle lanterns bobbing dimly in the dark as they set off for Cockermouth.

Using his pack as a pillow, Henry found himself lurching uncomfortably to and fro. For a bad moment he felt sick but it passed as everything began to settle to a more even roll.

They reached Caldewgate and splashed through the shallows, hardly two inches now, safely below the belly boxes.

Satisfied all was well, George strode out alongside at the front, half-seen in the dark, a guardian figure. Horses were his passion, horses and ghosts. About twenty-four miles to go. He wanted to reach Cockermouth early and claim a pitch in the town centre.

Henry's sleeping thought was a happy one. As the van swayed he pretended there was a girl at his side and they were flying through the air on a trapeze. He was unsure who she was but she was certainly beautiful.

Snivel was equally happy. Inside the caravan he reached out to douse the lamp, then changed his mind. Joey had not yet come to bed and there was time to do a little exploring. He began looking inside cupboards and drawers.

He was astonished. There was everything he could imagine – knives and forks, plates, cups and saucers, drawers of tools, bottles of beer, paper and pencils, scissors, clothes, even a sewing box. In among it all lay a threepenny bit coin. He pocketed it. No one would miss it.

Raiding the food cupboard he made himself a cheese butty. Just how did folk get to live in a caravan? He'd get one himself one day. That's what he'd do!

Behind a curtain in a corner he found a small cupboard. It held a surprise. Standing on a shelf was a tiny glass statue. It was about ten centimetres tall, a slender figure of a girl in a flowing gown. Such a small face and tiny delicate hands clasping a flower. Snivel had never seen anything so beautiful. It was so fragile that he hardly dared to hold it.

He opened a matching cupboard on the other side. Nothing but a long green purse. But it rattled invitingly. He opened it and marvelled. It was full of gold coins! Intrigued, he spread them out and lined them in rows on the table like little lines of soldiers.

Voices sounded outside.

Snivel turned rigid. In a panic he swept the coins back into the purse.

The statue!

Blindly he thrust it under the mattress of the nearest bunk and threw himself onto his own bed.

Whoever was outside had stopped on the steps and was talking. It was Joey! Snivel doused the lamp and lay listening.

Minutes passed before the clown came in. The man did not bother about a lamp. Snivel heard him dragging off his clothes and dropping them to the floor. The clown collapsed onto his own bunk and sank into the covers. For a while everything was silent then gradually Joey's snores began to fill the caravan.

His heart pounding, Snivel lay in the dark, his eyes wide open, frightened at what he had done.

16

Reluctant Patient

A worn rope handle was to blame. Annabel was crossing the farmyard at Dublands carrying a bucket of pigswill when the handle broke and sent her tumbling. Her cries for help brought Edgar and Jenny at a run.

"Nay, Annabel, what's going on?"

She lay in an awkward heap. "Get me up! I've twisted my leg."

The farmer tried to lift her.

"Edgar, stop! Oh, my goodness."

Her face turned white.

Jenny said: "Perhaps we can lift Miss Stalker between us?"

"I don't want your interference," snapped Annabel. But she couldn't get up.

"Fetch a chair from the kitchen, lass," said Edgar.

Despite Annabel's agonised glare, Jenny and the farmer lifted her onto a chair and carried her into the house. Jenny hurriedly made a pot of tea, and the warmth from the range and the drink gradually helped.

Edgar said: "Let me have a look." He felt gently round her ankle. "It feels like one of the bones is brokken."

"Brokken? Nonsense! It's nobbut a bruise."

"You need the doctor."

Annabel was having none of that. "We're having no doctor! He'll take every penny we've got."

"Of course he won't."

"I isn't having him!"

"Aye? Then show me how you get on. Try putting your foot down."

She glared angrily as if she would do no such thing, then changed her mind and took hold of the kitchen table and stood up. The attempt ended in a pained gasp.

"Thought so! We're going to see Dr Benson."

Edgar went and got the pony and trap ready. "We'll use the chair again," he told Jenny. Despite fresh protests from the patient, they carried her out and lifted her into the trap.

"Jenny, sit in the back will you and keep her company?"

Annabel looked bleak. "I don't need no one sitting with me," she snapped. Jenny didn't fancy sitting there either, but she said nothing.

Annabel glowered. "If we're going to town, then get the shopping bag. I'm not going to waste the visit."

Edgar sighed and went inside. Jenny wondered yet again how he put up with his difficult sister.

Jenny dragged on a coat and at Edgar's insistence climbed in at the back. Annabel did not stop talking, though Jenny decided that a broken bone would make anyone want to complain.

The trap and its reluctant patient set off down the lane leading to Cockermouth. None of them gave a thought to the date.

17

Don't Lose The Change!

Edgar frowned as he kept the pony and trap going. Cockermouth was less than half a mile away and unexpectedly the road was alive with horses and carts and people walking into town.

Annabel snapped: "We'll never get through this lot! I knew we shouldn't have come."

Jenny groaned. Why couldn't Annabel stop complaining?

The traffic was a puzzle until Edgar remembered the day. "Of course, it's Cockermouth hirings! Today's Hiring Monday."

It was a long crawl before they turned out of the traffic and reached the doctor's. Then things happened quickly. Annabel was carried into the surgery. A careful examination told the doctor all he needed to know.

"Broken tibia, just above the ankle by the feel of it. We must get you to the hospital."

Annabel protested: "I'm not paying for no hospital!"

"If the doctor says we go to hospital, we go," said Edgar testily.

Another struggle took place as they lifted Annabel back into the trap. Already it was one o'clock.

Jenny said: "If you don't mind, I'll follow on foot."

Edgar was surprised.

"I can shop a bit . . . I mean, we've no flour and things." She stood, straight backed, looking confident, and seeing this he leaned down and handed her a two-shilling coin. "All right. We'll be at the hospital. You'll be able to catch up with us there."

The trap was beginning to move away.

"The shopping bag!" cried Annabel. "Give her the bag!" A screwed up object came flying out into the road. "And don't lose the change!"

Jenny set off downhill towards the shops, and suddenly she felt gloriously free.

The town centre took her by surprise. Organ music and excited talk filled Main Street. Fairground stalls and show booths stretched from one end to the other and through this noisy tangle a slow river of people was moving.

Despite the crush, she got into a baker's and bought two loaves; then she moved on to the greengrocer's and the shopping bag was soon full.

Main Street was almost impassable. Now she must find the hospital.

"Jenny! Jenny!"

She got a better grip on the shopping.

"Jenny!"

She heard her name but did not immediately connect it with herself.

"It's me . . . Henry!"

At the same time a loud voice of a showman rang out: "Step up, step up! Give the missis a fright! Don't miss the Ghost Show!"

18

A Ghoulish Grin

The strange figure coming towards Jenny was wearing a bright yellow and green tunic with weird puffed out sleeves. Stranger still, his face was streaked with green and gold stripes.

"Whatever's happened to you!" she cried.

Henry grinned excitedly. Their meeting could not have been luckier.

"I'm working! At Biddalls. See! At the Ghost Show."

He waved at the glittering theatre behind him.

"But Aunt May wrote you were getting work in Carlisle!"

"I did, with the Ghost Show!"

His face shone.

"Come on and see us! It's great! And I can get you in for nowt!"

Jenny was pleased to see him. She stared at his strange costume and grinned. He looked crazy! Momentarily she was tempted, and then she remembered Annabel. "I can't. I've to go to the hospital. My employer's had an accident."

"Aw, come on! It's real scary."

"No, I really can't"

"You'll really like it!"

She shook her head. Sometimes he just didn't listen.

Henry smiled. She was fourteen now, and attractive. The girl of two years ago was already starting to change. He eyed her blue pinafore dress where it was beginning to tighten across her chest and wondered if she were still bossy, she had been when she had lived at Fingland. Even so, he was impressed.

Less obviously, so was she. Henry, still a bit lean, sixteen now, nearly seventeen and in a way still a bit young, though long trousers made him look more grown up, or would if he hitched them up properly. But he still had the same confident look that she liked.

There were only minutes to the next show. "Quick, tell us, did you get a doctor's place?"

"No, I'm on a farm. Stalker's, up at Dublands. But how long are you here?"

"Only till tomorrow. We got here this morning, from Carlisle and we were open by nine. It was a terrific rush! We're going to Workington . . . but I'll come and see you."

"How can you?"

"Dunno. Not now. But I will, Dublands. I'll remember."

Jenny stared at the glittering Ghost Show. She would have given anything to stay.

Henry said: "I'm sorry about your mum."

She looked down. Her mother's death still hurt. "It seemed to happen so quickly."

"What about your dad?"

She shrugged. "He's back at sea."

"I'm sorry." He wasn't good at this. He changed the subject. "We did a show for the workhouse kids this morning. Free. Really scared 'em.

You ought to meet George, Mr Biddall. He's great! A real showman. Everybody likes him."

For an instant he almost asked her the thought uppermost in his mind, but there was the sound of a harmonium and the opportunity went.

"Henry!"

A small green painted figure was yelling and waving up and down at the side of the theatre.

"We're starting . . . I gotta go."

"Who's that?"

"Snivel. He's my pal."

He hurried across the road, glanced back, gave her a ghoulish grin, and disappeared inside.

She stared at the gold lettering emblazoned across the top of the theatre: *Phantospectra Biddall's Ghost-O-dramas!* And elsewhere: *Fiery demons! Dancing skeletons.*

She stared enviously. She had to go.

Inside the theatre Snivel said: "So who's that then? Is that the one? Your girl?"

"Yes. That is . . . not exactly."

Dismally Henry knew he had still not asked her. What was the matter with him?

"She looks all right," said Snivel. "I tell ya, you're good at it, aren't ya? Chatting up girls."

"Course I'm not."

Snivel smirked. "She's nothing like your other 'un."

"Other one? What other one?"

"Zella."

"Gerroff! She's not my girl. None of 'em is."

"She keeps looking at ya. I tell ya."

The harmonium swelled. The wailing tones of *Phantom in the Workhouse* filled the crowded theatre; one by one the Biddall ghosts began to float up through the floor. Hurriedly Henry prepared the gingerbread sales tray ready for the interval. Snivel could be a pest at times.

Jenny arrived at the hospital and found Edgar sitting on a bench in a corridor.

"Brokken a bone in her ankle. She's having it put in plaster."

"Will Miss Stalker have to stay in hospital?"

He gave a weary smile. "She's refused! She wants home again. She's not going to like it but I'm going to have to telegraph Maud, her sister, to do the nursing. Now there's a trouble maker if ever there was one!"

Jenny hesitated. "But Mr Edgar, I can nurse Miss Stalker for you. I know how. I nursed my mum when she became badly."

Edgar smiled his thanks. "Well, it will certainly help until Maud arrives."

They left. The hubbub of the fair filled the town. Jenny wished she could go back to Main Street, if only for a few minutes, but there was no chance of that now. Such an exciting din!

19

Death On The Highway

All day Monday the ghosts wailed and screeched. For show after show the theatre was full, and there was no chance to rest; just time for snatched mugs of tea and a quick butty. Not until evening came was there a lull. Between eight and ten o'clock, almost uncannily, the crowd seemed to disappear, but as Henry began to think it was over for the day a noisy rush started all over again. Men began to pour out of the pubs. Beery men. Raucous. They joined their wives and children who had been standing in the streets waiting for them. The tempo of the fair picked up. It boomed on until midnight was striking.

Then almost abruptly it ended – though not silently.

Noisy hammering filled Main Street. From one end of Cockermouth to the other naphtha lamps fizzled and flared as the showmen and women dismantled stalls and sideshows. The speed this time took Henry by surprise. Some shows were already leaving and the Biddalls were aware of it.

"No rest, I told you." called Uncle Victor. He hurried past carrying a skeleton.

Selina waved. "Next stop Workington."

"But isn't that fair on Wednesday?" said Henry, puzzled. "It's just Tuesday now."

"Wednesday, yes. But this street has to be cleared by eight this coming morning – so we go now. Sometimes we go on to Maryport but not this time"

Four men dismantled the theatre and Henry saw how it had fitted together. Each section had a number and was stored methodically.

Caught up in the rush, the lads carried gnomes' heads to Joey at the belly boxes.

"How far's Workington?" Henry wanted to know.

Joey said: "About eight miles. All right if we go soon."

Selina signalled to Henry and Snivel. "Come on you two. Sleep."

Henry's turn in the bunk. He stretched out. What a treat! Somewhere distantly he heard George call: "Right, let's away."

The drivers yelled encouragingly at the horses. Sparks flew off the cobbles, chains clashed; slowly the Ghost Show wagons began to lurch out of town. Mander's Royal Waxworks followed and after them others joined in – the boxing booth, the fat lady, the shooting galleries, until a long line of horse-drawn vans stretched into the night. Soon Main Street and its fine houses were left behind. The town's citizens started to catch up on their sleep.

George was pleased. Business had been good. He locked up the big tin box with its precious earnings. He had always liked Cockermouth. He regarded it as his hometown. The townsfolk treated the Ghost Show well.

Henry woke abruptly and for a moment he couldn't think why. It was still night. Then he realised that the caravan was no longer moving. He waited for it to set off again and when nothing happened he went out and stared into the dark. He was surprised. The whole line of caravans had stopped. What was happening?

Distantly to the west the sky above the town of Workington shone with an eerie red glow from the steel works, but close at hand in the road there was a cluster of lanterns and the sound of voices. He went to look and Joey told him the news. Skipper, one of the two horses pulling the leading wagon, had stumbled. Before anyone could call halt, the Shire had crashed to the ground, dragging Nelson down with him.

Henry pushed to the front to get a better look. Rudge was struggling to free the reins as Nelson started to kick out.

"Hold this," Rudge ordered. He shoved a leather trace at Henry.

He grabbed it and held on tightly.

It took time to release Nelson. The other horse, Skipper, lay on the road.

"Is he all right?" asked Henry. He almost dare not look. Skipper lay ominously still.

"He's dead," said Rudge.

George and Uncle Victor came through. "Rudge, what's happened?"

"It's Skipper, boss."

"Oh, not Skipper!"

The giant horse lay crumpled, his eyes bulging as if his last few steps had been an ordeal. Henry could hardly look.

More folk arrived with lanterns. Worn faces seemed to crack a little as they saw the fallen creature.

George knelt and felt Skipper's head. "Now then, lad. What's this? You've not gone on us?"

His voice was strong and quiet but his words had no effect. Skipper's heart had stopped beating.

Uncle Victor said: "Skipper was one of the best."

George closed the horse's eyelids and stood up. Rarely did the showman lose his composure but for this one moment his face seemed to become a little older.

"We'd best turn off the road, lads. We need to get him buried."

A great sadness came over Henry. He moved away, a lump in his throat.

Workington was forgotten. The Ghost Show wagons pulled onto the verge and allowed the string of following vans to rumble by. Passing faces caught the lantern light as people stared. It was something Henry would never forget.

The Biddalls set to. Spades and a sling were pulled out from under a van, and while this was taking place George walked off alone into the dark. To George horse was king.

When he returned his face was calm again. He said simply: "There's a wide patch of grass alongside the road further back. It'll be a good place."

It was hard ground, by a forked ash. Rudge and another man set a pair of lanterns hissing on the turf and began to dig a trench, others joined them, working in relays. As the hole grew larger Henry and Snivel glanced at one another.

"Come on," said Henry, as the men paused. They clambered in unbidden and started to throw out the stones. Soon others joined them. It was tiring work and dawn was coming before George decided the hole was deep enough. Two more horses, Prince and Bill, were led up and the sling was looped round Skipper.

"Get on there!" yelled Rudge. "Heave!"

Prince and Bill dragged Skipper's heavy body along to the pit. As it reached the edge the show folk came forward and symbolically each one set a hand on the dead horse's back. Henry and Snivel paused uncertainly then caught an approving nod from Rudge. Henry did the same, waving Snivel to join him. At a signal from George, Prince and Bill took up the strain again and as they hauled at Skipper everyone kept a hand on the horse's body and helped to push. Skipper slipped out of the harness and went down into the hole with a thump.

Goodbye, whispered Henry.

The diggers started to shovel in the debris until the hole was full and they had levelled it off. They moved back to the caravans and prepared to leave.

"No man had a better worker," said George.

Uncle Victor told the boys: "Many a horse lies buried alongside these old roads did people only know it. Some men don't bother and sell the carcass, but not George. Not always. We lost another good one up in Scotland once and left it for someone else to dispose of it, but there was a lot of bother so if we decide to bury 'em we do it ourselves now."

A small figure was at Henry's side. It was Mr Lodge. The old man's face looked careworn. "You lose a loyal friend when you lose a horse."

"I've never seen a dead one," Henry told him.

"It's not a happy thing," said the old man sadly. "I've seen it happen twice before."

"Have you been on the road a lot?" asked Henry.

Mr Lodge laughed. "All my life."

He turned up his collar. The wind was growing sneaky.

"If you lads get chance come and have a mug of tea."

Henry promised they would. He had known these show folk only a short time but he was growing attached to them. Some were rough looking and swore a lot but they all got on with the job, working quickly. He envied the way they could just set off and travel not knowing what might happen next.

In the early hours, the Ghost Show pulled into Workington. To Henry's surprise George seemed to be in good spirits. The showman noticed his expression.

"Now then, lad, no need to stay miserable. Skipper had a good life. Rudge couldn't have treated him better. None of us could."

Henry reddened: "It's just how everyone seems so cheerful."

"On with the show, lad! On with the show! And see, here we are now . . ."

He might have said more but the showman's craggy face became tense. They had reached the Cloffocks showground and something was wrong.

20

Trouble At The Fair

George glared across the Cloffocks. "Someone's setting up on our pitch!"

Henry turned and saw Mander's Waxworks pulling in, but George was looking the other way towards the head of the paddock where men were putting up a pair of swingboats.

Uncle Victor exclaimed: "They've taken Mr Lodge's place as well!"

"Oh have they!"

George pulled down the neb of his cap and marched across.

"Now lads," he called. "What's all this about? You're on our pitch."

A solid looking man turned and scowled. He was short and broad chested, his hair black and ragged. "Your pitch is it? Well we heard you wasn't coming!"

Henry, at the edge of the group, felt a pang of alarm as the man took hold of a sledgehammer handle.

"Oh, did you?" said George. "And who told you that? We always have this pitch, along with Mr Lodge and his Aunt Sally."

"Now ain't that too bad," sneered the man. "Happen we are looking for a bit of trouble?" He edged menacingly at the showman.

But George did not flinch.

Henry marvelled. He did not know how the showman could just stand there. He was glad to be on George's side.

"There'll be no trouble; only common sense," said George calmly.

The dark haired man's hand tightened on the handle. Everyone was becoming tense. Henry looked down and bent to pick up a stone.

It was now that the simplest of things happened. Slowly, almost casually, members of the Biddall's team began to walk across the turf. Three at least were strong looking, with Rudge among them. They came and stood with George. A chill of excitement went through Henry. But that was not all. Other men were starting to join them from Manders. It was happening quietly until eleven showmen confronted the swingboats men.

"You'll be able to set up a bit further away, I'm thinking," said George.

The intruders seemed to be standing their ground.

Quietly, Rudge said: "We can do this peacefully or we can do it the other way."

That seemed to do it.

"Just a mistake, just a mistake," blustered the man. He spat at the ground.

"Take your time," George said agreeably. "We'll not rush you."

The swingboats men turned away, cursing under their breath.

"Ain't they gonna fight us?" said Snivel, disappointed.

"Course not," said Henry. He dropped the stone. "George isn't like that."

That much he knew already.

Snivel crouched like a boxer and punched his fists to and fro. "We could beat 'em easy!"

Uncle Victor said: "Some blokes will fight, even if one inch of their site's been pinched."

Henry wandered away, lost in a stream of thought. It was a pity Jenny had missed seeing the show, if only for a couple of minutes. He reckoned she could easily have stayed. And now there was Zella, well no there wasn't, not really; but she *was* fascinating. And how did she fly? Thinking this, he realised they would soon be preparing the ghost set-up. If he waited around the theatre she might be there and he could find out how it was done.

But Joey way-laid him. "I've been looking for you. In fact both of you. We've managed to clear all the stuff from one of the bunks, so you've got a bunk each tonight."

Henry and Snivel were relieved. Anything would be better than a belly box.

George let half an hour pass before he signalled work to begin. Several local labourers had been hired and they joined the Biddalls, helping to set up the two-wagon fronted theatre – the Flash, they called it. It was heavy going and there was a lot to do. Alongside the theatre they helped to erect Mr Lodge's Aunt Sally.

Henry and Snivel, not knowing where anything went, were given paintbrushes and squatted on the ground, surrounded by tins of paint and six of the gnomes' heads from the front of the stage. They set about repainting them, reddening their lips and cheeks and brightening their eyes.

The rest of the day passed quietly enough and the theatre was set up ready for an early start on the next morning.

21

A Rotten Thief

Workington sprang to life. Mid-morning and already people were streaming into the Cloffocks. Thunderous music poured from four rival organs, all competing with one another, and through this cacophony sounded the cries of the barkers and the crowd's excited yells and shouts.

It couldn't have been busier. Every performance of the Ghost Show was full.

Uncle Vic waved a hand. "As good as Cockermouth, hey?"

"You bet!" said Henry. Gingerbread sales were brilliant. Once again there'd hardly been time to snatch a sandwich. Hardly time for a drink.

By teatime seventeen Ghost Show performances had taken place. Not until five was striking did the crowd thin and a break come.

Tired out, the lads flopped on the grass. Snivel got out a bag of biscuits and they shared them.

"That old bike . . . how did you pinch it and no one see you?"

Snivel looked up proudly. "Dead easy! The old geezer never locks his shed. I just wheeled it out."

"You oughta be careful," said Henry. "The cops will get you."

"Yeah, well, folk leave stuff lying around and I sort of picks it up. Pinched me dad's false teeth once and hid 'em in the bread bin. He didn't half wallop us."

Henry grinned. "My dad would have done the same."

"When did your dad die?"

"Long ago now."

In fact it was six years. For a moment Henry felt a stab of loneliness. He remembered his dad with pride, and daft though it seemed one of the things he remembered was his dad's well-polished boots. Every night at bedtime his dad had set them on the bottom step of the stairs, side by side, as if they were on guard while everyone slept. Henry had always felt safe and glad they were there.

"So where's your mum, then?" said Snivel.

"At Fingland. She looks after a house for a friend."

His mother had married a second time but that had not worked out and she had left Silloth and gone to Fingland.

He changed the subject and took another biscuit. "Where'd you get these? They're good."

"The biscuit stall."

Henry stared appreciatively at the bag. Then the truth dawned. "You've pinched 'em!"

Snivel looked indignant. "Nay, I 'aven't! I've bought 'em."

"Bought 'em? What with? You've no money!"

Snivel went white.

Henry snatched the bag off him.

"But I did! I found a threepenny-bit," protested Snivel.

"Oh, yeah? And I know where. In the caravan!"

Henry was furious.

"You're a rotten thief! You've to give the money back."

"But I can't!" wailed Snivel. His voice seemed to turn to a squeak. "I-I's spent it."

Henry glared. "When George pays us," he said menacingly, "you go and give it him. And I'll make sure you do."

For the first time Snivel looked anxious. "Hey, you'll not tell 'em, will ya? I mean, not George."

"What else have you got?" Henry demanded.

Snivel didn't answer. Then he fished in his trouser pocket and handed over a leather packet. Inside was a pair of scissors. "I've not pinched 'em, I've only borrowed 'em."

"What the heck do you want these for?"

"S-so I can cut me hair."

"Your hair? Oh, do you! Well stop where you are, right now!"

"What?"

"Sit still!" Henry ordered fiercely.

Snivel, startled, did as he was told.

"I'll give you a haircut. Free." He eyed Snivel's ragged head and took hold of a lanky lock.

"Gerroff," protested Snivel. "I've changed me mind. I don't want it cutting!"

Henry forced him down. He would teach this titch a lesson. He chopped off a first lump.

"Hey, stop! Watch what you're doin'."

Henry smirked. "There's nowt to it."

Hair tumbled to the grass. It took no more than minutes. He trimmed a wisp end away.

"Now give 'em back."

He handed Snivel the scissors.

"Give 'em to Joey," ordered Henry sternly. "Tell him you found 'em on the caravan floor."

Snivel bit his lip. Henry was being tough, but he knew he was getting off lightly. He put a hand on his head.

He squawked.

"What 'ave you done? You've cut it all off!"

"No I haven't. You've lots left, and it'll grow again."

From now on he'd keep stricter watch on young Snivel. But would the titch ever learn?

Uncle Victor signalled to them. They returned to the theatre, and spread fresh sawdust on the ground. People started to come in, the seats filled, the ghosts began to reappear.

22

Zella

At last, midnight. The fair had wound down. Henry set a flickering paraffin lamp on the ground and began packing the pile of hay behind the theatre into large bags ready for loading.

In the gloom he failed to notice the figure approaching and was startled by a faint cough.

It was Zella.

"Hello?" she said softly. "I hoped I'd find you."

Surprised, he stepped back, conscious of her nearness, but she came closer. He was startled as he felt her body press against him. For a moment Henry was embarrassed, then she brought her mouth to his and their lips found one another. As they kissed there was a faraway sound of voices, but they heard nothing of them. In all the showground there was only the two of them.

Henry sought to move but Zella still held him closely. "S-sorry," he muttered.

"Sorry?" Her voice came in a whisper. "But I wanted to kiss you. Didn't you want to kiss me?"

He floundered, not knowing what to say.

"Are you surprised?"

"No, I mean . . . yes."

Help, that hadn't sounded right. He stood awkwardly as Zella realised the truth.

"Why, I don't believe you have ever kissed a girl before, have you?"

"Of course I have," he lied, but he said it too quickly.

"I don't believe you! I can tell. A first kiss!" She tried to see his face in the gloom and marvelled. She spoke softly. "How wonderful! But you know it can't go further, not ever. You're a nice boy . . . and I'm glad to have met you, truly, but it's only for now."

Henry still did not know what to say, but his senses were racing.

"Now I must go. We'll be setting off soon."

"No, wait . . . "

But she slipped from him and he was left standing, excited and astonished. Beautiful, beautiful Zella! Compared with her he knew that he was nobody and she . . .

His thoughts tumbled in a heap as it came to him what had happened. What had come over him? Somehow he should never have kissed her. Not Zella. But oh, how lovely she was.

Caught in thought, he picked up the lamp, not noticing a figure moving quietly away in the dark.

23

On The Road

Four o'clock in the blackness of night, the horse-drawn wagons lumbered south towards Whitehaven. They travelled noisily, dark shapes on the uneven road, the drivers grumbling as wheels bumped through potholes. Wednesday was behind them; they were intent now on reaching Whitehaven early so they could get pitches in the town centre.

The Ghost Show had split up. Mr Lodge's wagon had been slow to load and George had set off from Workington without it, with seven miles or so to go.

The boys travelled with Mr Lodge. Snivel lay inside, asleep on a bunk, and Henry was sitting on the driver's seat, enjoying travelling in the dark.

"What happened to me-laddo's hair?" asked the old man.

"I cut it," said Henry. Then wanting to change the subject: "Have you always been a showman on the open road?"

Mr Lodge shook the reins. "Since I was eight. My father had a barrel organ on little wheels, and we pulled it from fair to fair. He cranked the handle and played the tunes, and I'd collect the pennies in a cap. I used to like the *Roll Out the Barrel* tune best. I was thirteen when he died and Uncle Sam sold the organ. Then I got me own show. I was sixteen and earned eleven pence on my first morning!"

Henry was intrigued. "The Aunt Sally?"

"No, no." The old man smiled proudly. "I was a puppeteer. I had my own puppet theatre. Built it myself and Uncle Sam and me spent all winter making puppets. Carved 'em out of wood. There was Sweet Sally Teardrops, pretty as a fairy. The children loved her! And Smarty Pig, all pink and fat; Blinker, who pretended he couldn't see things unless it was a jam pudding. And there was Big Ears and Nasty Grasper.

"I loved 'em all and they seemed like they was real people. I'd lie in my bunk at night and think I could hear 'em talking to themselves in their box. And perhaps they did."

Henry was captivated. "But where did you go?"

"Everywhere . . ."

The old man gave a shiver. The night was starting to feel cold. "What about me making a pot of tea? Can you manage the reins?"

Henry took hold. It was a proud moment. He had never driven a horse before.

It was daylight when they arrived at Whitehaven. With three of them at work, the Aunt Sally was erected in record time. The port's streets began to fill. The rush began.

24

Jenny Sees Red

Trouble arrived at Dublands amid a clatter of hooves. It was hardly half-past eight when a pony and trap pulled up in the farmyard. Before anyone could properly stir, a short stiff woman in a black coat and bonnet was at the door and marching in.

The thin face of Annabel's sister, Maud, stared round appraisingly.

"Annabel! What's all this nonsense?" She slotted an umbrella firmly into a stand. "Brokken your knee, I hear? What have you been getting up to? And who's this? Not another new servant girl!"

Jenny found herself included in the glare.

Annabel looked annoyed. "Maud, you have no need to come bothering. Everything's all right. And it's not my knee, it's my ankle."

"Splendid! Then you can thank the Good Lord for being merciful," retorted the newcomer. She removed her bonnet and thrust it at Jenny, waving at her to put it away.

"Edgar had no right to call you," said Annabel. "I have managed since Monday without your help, thank you."

"Rubbish! Show me how you manage your crutches."

"Well I can't properly, can I? I haven't got used to them yet."

"Exactly! Until you do, I am stopping! I should have come earlier."

Jenny groaned. Two of them at it!

Maud turned to Jenny.

"Come with me, girl. As I have decided to stay, you can show me round and I can make sure the place is being properly run."

Jenny glanced at Annabel who looked as if she were going to tell Jenny to remain standing where she was, but Maud waved at her to follow.

They entered the front parlour. At once the woman's face stiffened. "As I thought. Do you call this clean? This fireplace is a disgrace!"

She ran a finger along the mantelshelf and examined it for dust.

"Never touched! Where is my room?"

She stomped up the stone staircase. In the small bedroom she paused again, flicking back bedclothes. "These sheets are too large for the bed! And this bolster case is not properly ironed."

Jenny seethed. "Miss Annabel got me to change the room for her, so it's not my fault!"

"Is that so!" Maud stared hard into Jenny's face. "Well she can't do it for herself now, can she!"

They toured the house and Maud's criticisms never stopped. Jenny grew more and more upset.

A grim supper followed. Jenny to her surprise was ordered by Maud to sit at a side table and made to eat alone. The others sat at the big kitchen table. They had always eaten together until now. Edgar glanced across at her but said nothing. Come nine o'clock Jenny was glad to escape and go to bed. For the first time since her mother had died she wept into her pillow.

Next morning matters came to a head.

Maud steered Jenny out into the yard and looked into the nettie, the lavatory shed. She glared at the white wooden seat. "Disgusting! This needs emptying and given a proper scrub!"

"But Jenks does it!"

"The handyman scrubs it?" said an astounded Maud.

"No, I mean . . . " Jenny was confused. She meant that Jenks emptied it out, and that she did the scrubbing.

"Well *you* might call it clean madam, but I don't. So you can do it again."

Jenny lost her temper. The woman was impossible. "I suppose you want me to dig the muck out as well, and chuck it on the fields!"

Maud bristled with anger. "How dare you!" Her hand lashed out and gave Jenny a stinging blow on her face. Shocked, Jenny stumbled on the cobbles, almost falling.

Maud glittered nastily. "I'll thank you to do your job properly! As long as I am here you will do everything exactly as I tell you. Now go and start preparing lunch. At once! I am famished."

"Oh, are you!" Jenny's face filled with defiance. "Well get it yourself!"

She ran to the house and began to fling clothes into her trunk. She dragged on her coat and grabbed a satchel. Tears stung her eyes. How she hated this place. How she hated the sisters!

A troubled Edgar met her in the kitchen. He saw the red mark on her face.

"What's all this with you and Maud?"

Jenny grimaced and tried to avoid his gaze. "I'm sorry, Mr Edgar, I'm going! Please send my trunk to my aunt's. I've written you the address."

Edgar shook his head. "Nay, lass, you know you can't leave. Not till term time. And Annabel will be needing you once she's feeling better."

Jenny's mind was made up. "No one is going to treat me like Miss Maud. I am not stopping."

"And good riddance!" snapped Maud, coming in. She stood at the fire range, stiff and militant. "The girl is a good-for-nothing. I saw it the moment we met."

Edgar turned sharply. "Is that so! Well you can keep your nose out of this for a start! Young Jenny's a hard worker and . . ."

But there was no Jenny. Already she was out in the open, her heart pounding as she hurried across the cobbles, clutching her satchel. Somehow she would have to get back to her aunt's at Fingland . . . or perhaps to cousin Alice's in Keswick. She set off down the track. Yes, Alice's first. She was not going to stay a moment longer at Dublands.

Down the track, out of sight of the house, she slowed and tried to calm herself. She had done it now. Lost her job. Whatever would Aunt May say! Girls didn't dare quit their work places, not till term time. No one dare.

It was half a mile down to the main road. She arrived in a gloomy state, which even the silver waters of Bassenthwaite did not dispel. Running away like this she knew was terrible. What if the Stalkers tried to catch her? And what about Miss Bewley, supposing she told the police! Could she do that? Jenny clenched her teeth. She had accepted the yearls shilling, which bound her to Annabel for six months.

She turned south alongside the lake towards Keswick. Rightly or wrongly, she had done it now. Well blow them! Between them

Annabel and Maud would have made anyone run away, and the agent Bewley – well she was too fat to run anywhere!

She walked until she reached a signpost. One arm pointed north, back along the way she had come, towards Cockermouth. A second arm pointed south to Keswick. She would have to take care not to run into Miss Bewley but so what? As it was, Alice was going to have a surprise.

Jenny was thinking this as she came to a turning and realised that someone was in the road behind her. Following in the distance was the shambling figure of a man. She had not noticed him until now and for some reason she began to walk faster. Nothing to bother about, but she felt a stab of unease. At a curve in the road, she stepped quickly in among the trees and stood quite still, her heart pounding.

It was a tramp. He came slowly, heavily wrapped and bareheaded. He was limping, but sight of the man's face caused Jenny's heart to miss a beat. Ugly purple and black bruises scarred his cheeks. A frightening thought struck her. Was it the man who had tried to break in at Dublands? The bruising looked fresh. Jenny felt sure it was him. Almost without thinking, she touched her own bruised face.

She waited several tense minutes before daring to look out. The tramp had gone past and was heading towards Keswick. Jenny groaned. Just where she wanted to go! He was going to be in front of her all the way. There was nothing for it. She couldn't take the Keswick road.

She turned round and set off in the other direction. She would look for a job in Cockermouth, at a doctor's, just as she had first planned. That would be better.

Feeling more positive, she walked steadily, the glittering lake bright under a clear sky. What she needed now was someone to talk to, someone she knew. And then she remembered the fair was in Cockermouth, and Henry would be sure to help.

25

Finding Henry

But the fair had gone. Hot and bothered, Jenny stared in dismay along Main Street. She had walked almost five miles to Cockermouth hugging her satchel and now Main Street's wide expanse was empty.

Outside a baker's shop she stopped a woman laden with groceries.

"Nay, lass, the fair packed up and went! They go soon as it's over."

Jenny's heart sank. "I thought it would be here all week. It's the Ghost Show I'm wanting."

"Oh, aye. Biddalls. It might be at Workington. But you'll have a job catching them now."

Once again she was having to change her plan. She abandoned all thought of getting a job in Cockermouth; she decided to catch up with the fair. She didn't pause to think what might happen once there. She would just go.

But how much would it cost? Jenny counted the coins in her purse. Enough to get to Workington anyway. The rest was still in her trunk at Dublands.

There was the sound of hooves as a bread van drew up outside the shop. Of course! She had shopped at this bakers when Annabel went to the hospital. The horse and van gave her an idea.

She went in and bought a currant teacake; at the same time she asked the assistant if there were a coach and horses to Workington. Well there was, from outside the railway station. She might be lucky.

Jenny hurried out into the street. A shiver of excitement came over her.

But at the station the Workington coach had departed minutes earlier. Everything seemed to be against her! Well, if not a coach, then what about a train? It was a daring thought. She had never been on a train. But could she go on one all by herself? Young girls didn't do that sort of thing; well, not usually.

Before she allowed herself to change her mind she went to the ticket office. The next train was in half an hour. Single or return? Better get a return. There, she had done it. She was having an adventure!

Giddily, as if money did not matter, she went into the station café. Why not be a lady for once? She ordered a pot of tea and sat at an elegant cast iron table. Her shoes were dusty and her pinafore dress no longer looked well ironed, but feeling good was what mattered, and she did feel good. Her hair at least looked all right, hanging in a silky plait down her back.

A rumble of an engine sent her hurrying out.

She set off along the platform, peering into the compartments until she found one with a woman passenger.

Such excitement! Pink cheeked, she took a seat. Moments later they were off.

The woman gave her a smile. "You are travelling alone?"

"I'm going to the fair at Workington," said Jenny proudly.

"At Workington? Oh, my dear, are you? I'm sorry; I don't think the fair will be there. It's probably gone on to Whitehaven by now."

Jenny's hopes died. Gone? She gazed out of the window at the passing countryside. Taking the train suddenly did not seem quite so clever.

They went on talking but Jenny could hardly concentrate.

At Workington as the train pulled away she found a porter. Had the fair gone? Yes, to Whitehaven. Or it might have gone on to Cleator Moor.

Cleator Moor! Didn't anyone know where it was!

What time was the Whitehaven train?

The porter stared at her oddly. "It's just left, miss. You've just got off."

"Oh, no!"

Of course, she vaguely remembered the women talking about train times! She should have stayed on. How could so much go wrong in a single day?

Close to tears, she stood on the platform wondering what to do, go back to Keswick, or go on? She found the ticket office. It would take every penny she had but it seemed she had no choice. She bought a return ticket to Whitehaven.

There was a frustrating wait before the next train came in. She was beginning to think she should never have set out in the first place. She wasn't even sure now why she had. She had never felt quite so lonely.

26

The Bossy One

Jenny struggled through the jostling crowd, sidestepping the drunks. Whitehaven's streets were full of stalls and show booths, full of noise. The fair was in full swing. A man grabbed at her, grinning, shouting, but she ducked past and headed towards a line of caravans where there was less of a crush. She let some yelling boys go by and glimpsed a girl at a caravan door in a glittering white costume. Then opposite the Custom House at the heart of the fair she found the brilliant green and gold booth of the Ghost Show.

She stared at the theatre and paused. It was now that she was struck by uncertainty. Dare she go in just like that and ask to see Henry? What if he wasn't there? He might have left. She was wondering what to do when she saw a figure she recognised. She hurried across.

"Hello, you? Can you help me?"

Snivel turned, surprised.

"Sorry, you won't know me – I'm Jenny Atkinson. I saw you at Cockermouth. Have you seen Henry?"

Snivel stared round-eyed. "Yeah, of course. He's fixing the harmonium. It's gone and busted again." And then, realising: "Oh, aye, you're Henry's girl, aren't ya?"

"What?"

"You're his girl. He's talked about ya."

"Oh, has he?"

Jenny felt a rush of colour to her cheeks.

"You're the bossy one."

"Bossy? Me?"

"I mean . . ."

"Thank you very much!"

Snivel had a feeling he had said something wrong.

Jenny's face had turned blank. Bossy was she!

"How can I get to see him?" she said coldly.

To Snivel's relief a welcome figure appeared "Oh, Zella, hello. This is Henry's girl, Jenny Atkinson. Can she go inside and see him? Is that all right?"

Jenny recognised the newcomer. It was the girl in the glittering costume.

Zella hardly paused. Jenny Atkinson? Oh yes, so this was his girl was it? She stared hard and decided she wasn't all that special, though attractive enough. Well there wasn't time to spare.

"No one's to interrupt him while he's looking at the harmonium," she said firmly.

Snivel tugged at Jenny's sleeve. "We'll have to wait," he said apologetically as Zella disappeared into the theatre. "Take no notice of her. She's snooty sometimes but she likes us really, Henry anyway. I'll get him for ya."

"A harmonium?"

"It went wrong and he fixed it."

"Who's the girl?"

"Zella? She does all kinds of things. She's really clever. You'll like her."

Oh, will I, thought Jenny. I don't think so.

"But how the heck did you find us?'

Jenny told him, and in turn he described how the Ghost Show was going to stop in Whitehaven for three days and then go on to the old mining town of Cleator Moor, but after that it was all going to end because the Biddalls were going up into Scotland.

"One of the Biddall's blokes hurt his hand. That's how Henry got us jobs, him being good at fixing things. He'll be right pleased to see ya."

Jenny cheered up at that. She looked enviously at the ornate theatre. She had never been inside a fairground show.

A loud fanfare sounded.

Snivel's face lit up. "There! I teld ya. He's fixed it."

The music swelled and then sank away as a voice rang out.

"Step up! Step up! Biddall's Ghosts. Time for the fright of your life!"

"That's Joey," said Snivel. "He's our best clown! Come on, we can get in at the side – oh yeah, here he is."

Henry was surprised. He had passed an unspeaking Zella as he came out, and wondered what was the matter, and now he caught sight of Jenny. At once a feeling of guilt swept over him.

"G-goodness, Jenny, hello . . . I hadn't s-sort of expected you here."

Jenny's smile faded. Henry didn't sound all that welcoming.

"I got a train from Cockermouth," she said lamely.

"Oh, did you? I thought you were at Keswick . . . I mean I thought you were on a farm."

"Dublands," said Jenny. And, suddenly decided: "I'm going back tonight, to Keswick, that is."

For the second time since leaving the Stalkers she experienced a horrible feeling that she should not have come.

Henry saw her unease and floundered. "I was thinking . . . that is, I mean, I was hoping perhaps I might visit you. Perhaps on Monday. I mean, at your farm place."

He knew he didn't sound convincing.

"You can't!" broke in Snivel excitedly. "The show's at Cleator Moor on Monday."

"I mean Tuesday," said Henry quickly. He went red. This wasn't going well.

Snivel said: "It's nearly show time."

Henry glared. "I know. I know." He looked at Jenny's crestfallen face and suddenly felt angry with himself. What was the matter with him? Nothing like this had ever happened before. She really was special. She always had been.

"I shouldn't have come," said Jenny.

Henry took hold of himself. "Of course you should. Look, why don't you stop and see the show . . . then we can get to talk afterwards?"

Jenny was about to say no, but Snivel chipped in again and for once he told a helpful fib.

27

Not A Real Kiss

Snivel grinned at Jenny. "You gotta see our ghosts. They's brilliant! Henry's said millions of times how he wishes you was with us and could see 'em. You know, 'cause how you missed 'em at Cockermouth."

Jenny looked at Snivel and smiled.

For his part, Henry blinked. It was not exactly true, he had mentioned it once a while back, but looking at Jenny it was obvious Snivel had pleased her. He gave her a reassuring look. "Won't you stay and see the show? It's really good."

There were only minutes to the start.

Before she could answer Selina came by. "Henry, well done! I hear you've saved us again."

It was his turn to be pleased. "I was lucky. I mean I tightened it up a lot more this time."

She laughed. "You'll have to change your name to Biddall if you go on like this! But who's your friend?"

"This is Jenny."

There was no time for a proper introduction; the harmonium was about to play *God Save the Queen*.

Selina glanced at Henry approvingly and gave Jenny a smile. "You here to see the show? Then come and have supper with us after it's all over."

"I'm sorry," began Jenny. "I can't . . ."

Selina had gone.

"Now you've got to see it," said Henry. "But what about your job?"

"I lost it!"

"What?"

"I mean I ran away. No more farms for me, thank you. Now I must be going."

He shook his head. "But you can't miss supper. You're specially invited."

And suddenly at this moment more than at any other he knew what he wanted; despite everything, he wanted her to be his girl. Had done all along. The strange thing was, he had never yet dared to ask her. Nor had he ever kissed her, though he had been tempted.

"Must you go to Keswick tonight? I mean, you can stop with us! I'll see Selina. There's lots of spare places, so long as you don't mind being a bit squashed."

"Hey, come on!" yelled Snivel. 'You're going ta miss it!"

Jenny found herself propelled up the entrance steps.

"I don't believe in ghosts, you know . . ."

Whoosh!

As she entered the entrance tunnel into the show a white skeletal thing seemed to crash down at her. She gave a startled scream.

For the first time since her arrival Henry grinned.

The theatre was crowded. He hurried her down to the front benches.

"Squash in here till I get back. It's real creepy!"

Jenny found it more than creepy. It was scaring. Like magic, phantom figures appeared and disappeared. The clowns fought, accusing one another. A wondrous flying angel filled the theatre with startled "Ohhhhs!"

Jenny sat forward mystified. That looked like the Zella girl. How on earth could she just fly like that? She really did look like an angel . . .

So she liked Henry did she? Well that made two of them.

The final swirl of music sounded. The lads were back.

"Well?"

Jenny shivered. "It's brilliant! Really weird."

Snivel and Henry exchanged satisfied grins.

"I think I know how she does it," Henry confided. "Fly, I mean."

"But there's no wires."

"No. I'm going to ask her how it's done. Now we've gotta help with the next show . . . stop a tick with Sniv will you? I'll be back. You'll meet all the Biddalls! Or most of 'em anyway."

Snivel bounced alongside. "There's hundreds! Wait till you see Uncle Victor."

Henry went and found Selina. Quickly he told her what he had in mind. "Will that be all right? Just a day or two, till you leave?"

The little woman laughed. "And I was thinking you had your eye on Zella! Leave it to me. But I'll not let Jenny sleep in a belly box. Tell her if she likes she can help me with the supper."

Jenny did. While the ghosts howled she helped Selina peel potatoes and shell peas. Then they set the table in the big living caravan, and Selina told her about life on the open road and how the

Cumberland Run was famous all across the North and was the showmen's hardest working week in the whole year, with show after show, and how they had just lost one of their best horses, and everyone was feeling sad.

Gone midnight at last. Jenny stood in the gloom and watched the show-hands close up the front of the theatre. Soon Snivel and Henry returned.

"She's really nice."

"Zella?"

"No," said Jenny, "Selina."

"Yes, she likes you, I can tell," said Henry. "And Zella's all right, in a way, when you know her a bit."

Jenny felt nervous and excited. Zella was not exactly her kind of person. She might look like an angel, but she was a bit stuck up.

"Is she a Biddall?"

Henry looked surprised. "Yes, of course . . . she's George's wife."

"Not Selina, I mean Zella."

"Oh, Zell, no she's just here for now and works for the Biddalls, like some of the others. She's really good. Everyone likes her. She's going to be famous one day and become a great star."

So it's Zell is it, thought Jenny. She flicked her tress.

"She can down a beer in one sup," said Snivel enthusiastically. "And she's good at kissing."

"Kissing?"

"Yeah, I mean . . ." He shot a guilty look at Henry.

Jenny was startled. "She's kissed *you*?"

"Nay, not me," said Snivel hurriedly. Open mouthed, again he looked at Henry.

Jenny guessed the rest. "I see. So it's *you* she's kissed, is it?"

"Oh, wait! It wasn't a real kiss, I mean, I can explain," said Henry, knowing instantly that he couldn't.

He glared at Snivel.

"Don't trouble yourself," said Jenny. "Save your energy."

"It wasn't anything," said Henry. "She's not bothered about me one bit."

"Oh, isn't she? She just likes kissing you!"

Jenny was furious.

"I might have known. You're like all lads. You only think of yourself!"

"No I don't! You've got it all wrong," said Henry.

"Have I? I don't think so!"

She scowled angrily.

Henry lost his temper. "All right, if that's how you want it! See if I care."

He stomped off.

"Supper time!" yelled Selina.

28

A Brush With The Rats

Supper was an ordeal. Too late to refuse, Jenny sat through the talk and lusty singing pretending that everything was all right. She ignored Henry, something Selina noticed though she made no comment. Jenny was more than glad when Selina showed her to a spare bunk in a caravan. She lay awake thinking. Come morning she would catch the train and go.

Henry felt no better. He was regretting the way he had hurried away. And matters grew worse. Not until he got into bed did he realise that his precious watch, the one given to him by Ted, had disappeared. Dismayed, he searched through his clothes and the bedding, but it had gone. He had it last night, so where was it? Why was everything going wrong? First, Jenny; and now his watch.

Early next morning Jenny wandered alone in the fairground, scarcely noticing where she was going. She had helped Selina to clear up and wash their breakfast dishes, but she hadn't told her yet that she was going to leave. She wanted to go quickly without fuss. Ninety minutes more and she would catch the train to Keswick. She would escape from it all.

The fair was slow to start. People were beginning to arrive in dribs and drabs and a few of the smaller stalls and shooting galleries had already opened. She paused at the edge of a group of farmhands. A ragged man with a weathered face and an even more ragged woman were standing alongside a wooden tub of water.

A billboard announced:

> The Rat Tub
>
> GRAB THE GOLDEN SOVEREIGN!
>
> (Mouths only! No hands!)
>
> One penny a go!
>
> WIN A REAL SOVEREIGN
>
> Solid 9 Carat Gold

Glittering in the bottom of the tub lay a golden coin. Jenny could see it shining, but she could also see two black rats swimming about as if guarding it.

"Don't be frighted, lads!" bellowed the tout. "Bite up the sovereign. Defy the friendly rats."

Jenny shuddered. They were anything but friendly.

"Don't hang back, now!" The man hitched up his coat and glanced sharply up the street. "Lovely Aggie here will take your pennies."

Lovely Aggie opened her brown leather bag, which was as wrinkled as her face.

A broad shouldered youth handed her a penny. Not even pausing, he ducked his head into the water with a splash, and instantly yelled and pulled back. His face had collided with a rat.

The onlookers roared with laughter.

Others followed. One after the other the daredevils ducked in, and as quickly dragged out. Shrieks from their girls, sheepish grins from the lads.

"Come on young sirs! Win a golden sovereign. Only at the Rat Tub."

Jenny was beginning to move away when she realised that Henry was there in the crowd. He seemed to be eyeing the rat tub. Surely he wasn't thinking of having a go? Still annoyed with him, she kept well back, not wanting to be noticed. All the same, she waited.

Henry knew that she was there. He had seen her arrive and was avoiding glancing in her direction. He had been about to find Snivel but knowing Jenny was watching he changed his mind and moved closer to the tub.

He had realised that everyone ducked into the water with too big a splash. That way no one seemed to reach the bottom properly. Better to try and go in slowly, if only he dared.

Jenny put a hand to her mouth in dismay as Henry held out a penny. She pushed forward to get a better view. What if the rats bit him?

Henry fixed his eyes on the exact spot where the sovereign lay and blanked his mind to one thought: the sovereign was less than a foot away. He brought his face close to the water. The rats were swimming frantically round and round, desperate to get out. Holding his breath, he pressed down.

Slowly, now! Slowly!

His forehead nudged the bottom. He moved along until suddenly his breath failed. He pulled out in a rush to a chorus of whistles and jeers. He had missed the coin.

"Again," gasped Henry. "I want another go!" He held out another penny.

"Oh, ho! A brave lad here, lads and lasses! Thank you, young sir. The young sport is going to have another go, he is."

Again the tub man glanced along the street and Lovely Aggie watched the other way. Both seemed to be on edge.

The crowd was growing and for some reason Jenny noticed a small pale-faced man in a shabby raincoat moving through the crush close to her. She saw him pause, and move on, then stop again. Something seemed odd about his manner.

Henry saw none of it. He crouched at the edge of the tub and stared down. He would push straight at the sovereign this time; he had gone too far to one side. Taking a deep breath, he closed his eyes and pressed into the water.

A rat brushed his face. Don't panic! Something unpleasant scrabbled at his neck; a rat was at his hair! Keep going!

He moved across the bottom of the tub feeling for the sovereign. A moment later he found it. Blowing a stream of bubbles, he closed his teeth on the coin and in a rush dragged himself out.

"Yarrrrrrrrh!"

Startled cries rose from the crowd. As Henry's head came up, so did a black shiny body. Girls screamed as the rat tumbled to the ground and raced in among the onlookers' legs.

Henry gasped for breath, dismayed. In the rush the coin had fallen from his mouth.

The tub man shouted angrily. "My rat! You devil. You've lost my rat!"

Henry ignored him. Still breathless, he got onto his knees, searching the muddy cobbles.

"Let me help you, young sir." A small man in a shabby coat came down alongside. But Henry glared and pushed him away. "I'm all right!"

"No, no, young sir. Two will find it quicker."

The man was scraping at the mud.

Henry thrust the newcomer hard in the ribs.

"Get back or I'll thump you!"

He might have said more but a sudden sure voice rang out: "Henry, the sovereign! It's under the tub man's foot. His left one! He's just covered it over!"

Jenny was at the front of the crowd pointing at the tub man's boots.

"You keep out of this!" snarled the tout.

"You're hiding it," she cried. "You're cheating!"

Angry murmurs arose from the onlookers.

"I'm doing nothing of the sort!"

"Then move your foot!" cried Jenny.

Everybody heard her. Cries sounded. "Go on, mister, move it!" The crowd was on Henry's side.

"I know it's there!" cried Jenny, determined not to let him get away with it.

Scowling, the tout shifted his feet and Henry grabbed at the mud. He held up the sovereign.

The man moved as if to snatch it off him but the attempt was never made. A shrill cry sounded from Aggie.

"Giles! The cops! It's the cops!"

A glance at the crowd changed everything. Two uniformed constables were approaching.

The tub man grabbed up the remaining rat and stuffed it into a pocket. At the same time, the little pale-faced man was helping to tip out the water.

The police were a fraction too late. The trio was hurrying away, taking the tub with them.

Henry polished the sovereign on his shirt.

"Jenny, thanks . . . you saved it." A golden guinea! He looked at her and smiled.

Impulsively he held out the coin. "Go on, you have it. It's for you!"

But Jenny was still angry.

"No thank you! You can keep your money. I don't want it. And you can keep your Zella, too, for all I care!"

Henry's face fell. For a moment he had thought she wanted to make up.

"Are we not friends, then?"

She spoke sharply. "I'm catching the train home."

She turned away and hurried back to the caravan. Tonight she would stay with cousin Alice, and tomorrow would go home to Aunt May's. How she wished she had never left.

She tipped out her bag and set about repacking the few clothes she had brought from Dublands. She was relying on Edgar to send her trunk home with the rest of her belongings. As it was, the Ghost Show performances would start again soon and she was determined to leave before they did.

She reached for the train tickets. They were wrapped in a clean handkerchief, a return ticket from Cockermouth to Workington, and one from Workington to Whitehaven. She tipped everything onto a bunk. She tried her jacket pockets. Where were they? She searched through a second time. The handkerchief and tickets were not there. Dismayed, she felt in the pockets again and as she did so she realised with horror that not only had she no tickets, she had no money either. She had spent the last on her Workington ticket.

Dismally she flopped onto a bunk. Every penny she had was miles away in her trunk. Her heart sank. There was no one she could borrow from. Certainly not Henry. How was she going to get home?

For a moment she had a terrible feeling of being trapped, but perhaps there was another way. The Ghost Show was going to Cleator Moor on Monday, and after that up into Scotland. It would surely pass through Carlisle. That was the answer! She would ask Selina if she could have a lift. At Carlisle she would still have to get to Fingland, but she could walk the rest of the way. It was hardly nine miles. She'd done it before.

29

Stolen

Henry was still upset about Jenny. He was dithering whether to try and explain it was all a mistake. He guessed there would be a train soon and then she would be gone. He almost decided to go after her and tell her how he felt, but he abandoned the thought even as it came. It was the Ghost Show's busiest day.

A man emerged from behind a caravan. It was Kyle. He was short and stocky, one of the workmen. Henry had scarcely noticed him before except in passing, but he knew he wasn't a Biddall.

He surprised Henry, taking hold of an arm.

"So what ya doing?" he demanded. "Nothing, eh? Then grab that bucket and help me grease the wheels."

Henry shook himself free. "I've got to go somewhere."

"Have ya, now?" The man sounded sarcastic. "Well the wheels come first."

"But it's urgent."

"So are the wheels."

Kyle had jacked up a corner of a caravan and an iron-rimmed wheel already lay on the ground.

"You grease the axles as I get wheels off, and make sure you put plenty on."

Henry, annoyed at being bossed, looked for a brush. He had to be quick.

"What do I use?"

"Yer hands, what d'ya think ya use?"

A surge of anger swept Henry. He scooped up a handful of grease and stuffed it on the end of the axle. He'd kick this Kyle's bum if he dared.

"More than that!" snapped Kyle. "That won't last five minutes."

Henry dug deeper into the bucket and slapped a thick dollop on hard. The grease splattered to the ground.

Kyle swore and thrust him aside. "What the devil are ya doing? God knows why the boss bothers with you!"

Henry lost his temper. "Don't push me!"

He realised he was shouting.

Kyle's face turned crimson. "Push ya? I'll knock your ruddy block off."

A second later he might have done just that but they were interrupted by an approaching figure.

It was Joey. He was wearing his bright red and yellow clown outfit, though his expression was anything but cheerful.

He cast a troubled glance at Henry.

"Kyle, I want to speak to Henry."

The man glared. "Do ya, now? In that case don't bother bringing him back."

"Come on," said Joey.

Henry released his clenched fists. He knew Kyle could easily have flattened him.

"Let's get to the caravan," said Joey.

"Joey, I need to go," said Henry desperately. Jenny was probably already on her way to get a train.

"Sorry, it's important." He led the way to the van.

Frustrated, Henry sat at the table.

The clown asked suspiciously: "What was that all about?"

"I dropped some grease. We were doing an axle."

Joey's sad clownish eyes were fixed on him. Whatever was the matter? Henry could see that something was.

The clown didn't wrap it up.

"While you and Snivel have been sleeping here I'm sorry to say some things have gone missing. There was a little statue, a glass one. I wonder if you've seen it?"

Henry was startled. And immediately felt uncomfortable. He shook his head. "No, sorry, I haven't." And despite knowing Snivel had pinched a threepenny bit, he added: "And I don't think Snivel has either. He's never said owt."

Joey said: "It's a good-luck mascot. A glass angel. My grandmother gave it me when I was a boy."

He turned and opened a small cupboard behind the curtain. "It was in here the day you came. It's where I always keep it."

Henry stared, surprised. He had never seen behind the curtain.

"I didn't know there was a cupboard."

"Well it's not just the statue that's been stolen, some money's gone too."

He opened a second cupboard.

"There was a purse in here. That's gone."

Despite himself, Henry felt his face turning red. "Well it wasn't me!"

Silly though it seemed, Henry began to feel guilty.

"Are you certain you've not seen them?" Joey persisted.

"Of course I am," said Henry. His voice began to rise. "Joey, I wouldn't steal! Not from you, not from anyone. I wouldn't pinch a thing. Not ever!"

Joey didn't look any happier. Nothing had been solved. Only two days ago the boy had seemed so promising. Now he wasn't sure Henry was telling the truth, though there was another possibility. "If you've not seen them, what about young Snivel?"

Henry wiped his mouth on the back of a hand. He hardly knew how to answer. For a difficult moment he was silent and unable to look Joey in the eye. Had the titch done something stupid again? The lad needed his brain fixing.

The clown was aware of his hesitation.

"He wouldn't steal anything," Henry said at last. But he could tell that Joey was not convinced.

"Well I want to see him. If you lads haven't seen them, then someone else must know where they are."

Joey straightened the curtain. "I'm going to have to tell George. He doesn't like thieving. Be sure you bring young Snivel to see me."

Henry went out, deeply unhappy. He met Snivel coming up the field.

"Me and Rudge 'ave just fed the horses," said Snivel proudly. "He says I'm doing well. Tell you what – I wouldn't mind a nag of me own. One that'll pull me own caravan. When I get one!"

Snivel became aware of Henry's worried expression. "Hey, what's up?'

"It's Joey," said Henry. "He wants to see you."

"Me?"

"Summat about a statue. I told him we ain't seen one."

He was startled by Snivel's response: "Yeah, we have! I mean, I have. A little 'un. It was in a cupboard."

"A cupboard? He's real upset."

Snivel looked anxious as he remembered abruptly what had happened.

"I was only looking. I mean, I was going to put it back, but it went all wrong."

He was starting to become wheezy.

"Wrong?" said Henry. "What do you mean? Joey'll think we've pinched it! It was bad enough nicking the scissors and the threepenny bit. Now a purse full of money's gone too. We'll get kicked out."

Snivel's face turned white. "What d'ya mean?"

"Are you gormless? We can't stop with the Ghost Show, can we? Not if they think we've pinched owt."

Snivel's small face filled with dismay.

"But we haven't! I haven't."

The statue lay hidden under Joey's mattress. Why hadn't he put it safely back in the cupboard?

"So where is it?" asked Henry. "And where's the money?"

Snivel didn't answer. The purse! What had he done with it? Dismayed he realised it had been on the bed. But it couldn't still be there! It wasn't. He'd have seen it. Anyone could have seen it.

Henry, exasperated, said: "Come on! We've gotta see Joey."

Snivel seemed to grow a little smaller. He turned away from the caravan.

"Where are you going? He's waiting."

"I need a pee," said Snivel.

"Well hurry up."

Henry sat on a bin and waited impatiently. He had an uneasy feeling about the whole thing.

Minutes went by. Henry got up. Where the heck was Snivel? He couldn't be peeing all this time.

He went round the vans looking, but Snivel was nowhere to be seen. Alarmed, he hurried back to tell Joey.

Joey looked grave. "Has he run off?"

Henry didn't know. "I think he's scared."

Deeply unhappy, Henry set off again to search. A ghostly wail sounded; another show was starting. He looked everywhere he could think of, even in the empty belly boxes. It wasn't just that the titch had disappeared; Henry felt he was under suspicion himself. He could tell that Joey wasn't sure whether to believe him or not. What would Uncle Victor think? And where was Jenny?

Henry met Kyle.

"You again!' said the man. "Pinching stuff, are ya? Sneaking into vans?"

Henry was shocked. "No, we're not!" he retorted angrily.

"Aye, so why's the little devil run off?"

"Who says he has? Who told you?"

"We all know," said Kyle. "It's what comes of having outsiders around."

"The Biddall's lads are always around."

"Aye. But they are fairground folk."

Henry smarted.

"I'd 'ave thrown you out long ago."

Between shows, a meeting was called in George's caravan. Henry was not invited but he knew it was taking place.

George looked troubled. "He can't have gone far. Has everyone had a good look?"

They all said they had. Snivel had disappeared.

"He might be trying to walk back home," said Uncle Victor. "I'll take a look down the road."

George shook his head: "No, we've no time now. Ten minutes and we're on again. But there's another worry, a silver Christening spoon's gone missing from one of the other vans. It was little Anna's and was hanging on a string over the mantelshelf. And Pedder says his clock's disappeared, though that's not exactly a surprise."

Everyone knew about little Anna's spoon. She was one of the youngest children on the site. She loved the shiny spoon. As for Pedder, a handyman, well he was always losing things.

Selina said: "You don't really think it's the lads do you?"

Joey was unhappy. "Unless the money and statue are found it's hard to say. I don't know who else could be the culprit. We'd better do the gingerbread sales ourselves."

George got to his feet. "It seems we may have a thief in our midst. As it is, make sure the van doors are locked until bedtime."

120

They broke up.

"We're going to have to talk again," said George.

Uncle Victor looked grim. "I hope we don't have to tell them they've to go." He felt the matter more than any of them. He remembered how the lads had come to his rescue.

Henry saw them come out of the van. A few glanced his way, but none paused long enough to speak as they hurried into the theatre. What had they been saying? What should he do? He went back to Joey's van. An undertow of anxiety tugged at him.

30

A Small White Face

An hour later Selina found Snivel. She was peeling potatoes and carrots for the next evening meal. Gathering the scraps into a bucket, she went round to the waste tub by the hay pile and was tipping them in when she became aware that she was being watched.

A small white face stared at her from the depths of the hay.

"Oh, hello," she said. And then, casually: "Are you all right?"

The face didn't answer.

"We've been wondering where you were. Are you going to come and eat with us later?"

Still no response.

"We're having stew."

"I don't want none."

She nodded agreeably. "Oh well. It's just I need a bit of kindling. The stove's got very low."

Snivel's face flickered. He sniffed, and then sneezed abruptly as the hay got him.

"I don't suppose you know where it's kept?"

She knew that he did.

"A few sticks would do."

He wiped his nose on his sleeve. "It's behind Rudge's."

"Oh, then I'll soon find it." She sounded relieved, and paused.

Snivel didn't move. His face screwed up. "I'd get it for ya, but Joey will wallop us."

"Wallop you?" She sounded surprised. "Joey? Goodness no. He'd never do a thing like that! I'd not let him."

Her voice became reassuring. "Joey's a bit worried. He thinks you've got lost. Anyway, everyone's busy now with a show. Perhaps if you could fix the fire for me I'll make us a nice pot of tea?"

Snivel still stared and Selina began to move away.

He struggled out.

"I never got lost," he told her.

She nodded. He was so small. Such thin legs.

They collected a bundle of kindling from behind Rudge's and once back inside her van Selina boiled the kettle on the primus and made a pot of tea while Snivel fed sticks into the stove.

"I'd like me own caravan one day," he told her. "One like yours."

That made her smile. She wrapped her shawl round her shoulders. "They're good little homes. George and I love ours. We love to travel."

"Yeah."

She poured two mugs of tea and set them on the table.

"I'm right sorry we gotta go," he told her.

"Go? Go where?"

"Me and Henry. He says we must go, because of them things that have got lost. They all think it's us as got 'em."

Selina eyed him steadily, realising he knew more than he was saying.

123

"Surely you don't have to go? I mean, Joey seemed to go on about Henry, not you. I'm sure you can stop till Tuesday, till we go to Scotland. There's plenty to do."

He stared into his tea looking unhappy. "Aye, well, he's me pal. We keep together, like."

They sat in silence and Selina waited, and suddenly when he had been planning no such thing, it all came tumbling out, how he had found the statue, and before he could put it away properly, how Joey had come in and he had pushed it out of sight. And how he had found the money, but he hadn't taken anything. And he was worried in case the police were going to come and ask lots of questions.

He was looking scared.

"So that's why you ran off?" Selina said.

Snivel gave a hefty sniff. "I didn't run off really. I just wanted to hide a bit."

Selina nodded. She felt that way herself sometimes. A thought struck her. "What about us telling Joey you are all right? If you want I could tell him for you. He'll be glad if we do."

Snivel hesitated. A ghostly wail sounded distantly. Another show was ending. Somehow the eerie cry helped him to make up his mind.

"No, I'll tell him myself."

"Have some more tea," said Selina. She refilled his mug.

Twenty minutes later Snivel set off, nervous and apprehensive.

"Oh, hello," said Joey.

Snivel was at the open door of Joey's van.

"Come on in! We've been wondering where you'd gone."

Snivel didn't pause, for the second time in half an hour he blurted out what he had done.

Joey listened and did not interrupt.

"And I know where it is," said Snivel at last. "The statue, I mean."

Joey's bushy eyebrows rose. "You do? Goodness me, where?"

"But I never took any money," said Snivel. "And Henry didn't either. It wasn't him. It was me, and I didn't take owt. Honest! And I hid the statue."

Joey tilted his head quizzically.

"It's under there," said Snivel. He pointed at the bunk. "You come in that quick it was the only spot I could think of."

Joey was surprised. For a moment he didn't move, then he stood up and raised the edge of the mattress.

"Goodness," said the clown.

The light glinted on a cluster of bright fragments.

"I've been sleeping on it!"

Snivel's eyes widened in horror. The tiny statue lay in pieces.

Joey was silent.

Snivel was close to tears. "Oh, Joey, I'm real sorry!"

The clown picked up the bits and cupped them in the palm of a hand. "I guess I must have been a bit too heavy."

He looked sad.

"Will it glue?" said Snivel.

Joey shook his head. "Can't leave broken glass around. But I will keep a souvenir."

He picked out a fragment, a tiny hand holding a flower, and placed it on a shelf. The rest he dropped into a bin.

A voice sounded outside. "Are you there? We're starting again!"

"We must go," said Joey. "I think it's time we got on with some work."

The clown was suddenly matter-of-fact and practical. "What about your gingerbread tray? Got it ready? No? Then that won't do. We'd best not miss any sales. George wants to start, and I must tell him we've found the statue."

He gave Snivel a goofy smile and rolled his eyes. Suddenly Joey had become his old self again, Joey once more was Joey the clown. Snivel gave a sniff of relief. Perhaps everything would turn out all right.

31

Sunday Bakers

Saturday midnight, the final show in Whitehaven. A long day was over and Sunday here at last. Thankfully the tired Ghost Show gang put up the temporary boards till morning. They ate almost silently, bone weary, and soon folk began collapsing into their beds. It had been a long hard week not helped by the general air of unease among them. Could it be there was a thief in their midst? The missing money hadn't been accounted for.

Sunday dawned quietly. There was time now to pack everything away without having to rush. Soon they would be ready to set off along the road to the little town of Cleator Moor. Some were already leaving, keen to get a good pitch.

"We'll never catch up with 'em," said Snivel.

"Course we will . . . and stop picking your nose!"

"I isn't pickin."

"You are! You're always doing it!"

"Well, so do you!"

Henry, miserable over Jenny and feeling some still suspected him of thieving, resisted the temptation to bash him one.

Then he got a surprise. When he was least expecting it, he was startled to see Jenny coming out of Selina's caravan. So she hadn't gone after all! His hopes rose. Perhaps she had changed her mind.

The thought was short-lived. He paused as if to speak but she walked away, ignoring him. He was puzzled. Why was she still here? She was being snooty, that's what!

Jenny had known it was going to be difficult to keep out of Henry's way and was relieved when Selina had asked if she would help to bake a fresh supply of gingerbread. Almost all of it had been sold. They retreated into one of the big living vans.

The two of them got on well and Jenny soon felt more cheerful as they set to work. The oven was small and needed careful managing. She was good at keeping it going. She bided her time about asking for a lift, hoping the right moment would come.

"Couldn't help noticing," Selina remarked as the first tray load of gingerbread came out, "are you and Henry not talking?"

Jenny looked up in surprise. "Sort of."

Selina smiled knowingly. "It happens. Is it our dear Zella?"

Jenny flushed. "Well, not exactly . . ."

What could she say?

Selina waved a floury hand. She had observed Zella's glances in Henry's direction. "Zella's a lovely girl and very talented. George and I feel she's going to go far in life, but she can also be a bit thoughtless. I saw how you were ignoring the two of them."

Jenny smiled ruefully. "Didn't know it was so obvious. We've sort of had a quarrel, Henry and me." She trailed off, feeling awkward.

Selina rolled out another layer of gingerbread. "I'm afraid it's one of life's great truths, we're all human and make mistakes, but Henry's a good lad."

Jenny knew Selina was right, but it didn't quite ease her unhappiness.

The caravan filled with the aroma of freshly baked gingerbread.

"It smells delicious," said Jenny.

Selina was pleased. "So it should! We fairground folk have made gingerbread for hundreds of years. There were even gingerbread fairs. Mother used to make little heart gingerbreads for spring and all kinds of birds for autumn. As it is, I've made a special one, just for you!"

Selina smiled mischievously and handed Jenny a tiny ginger biscuit shaped like a man. "Be careful! It's a gingerbread husband. Nibble that and you'll risk meeting your future husband!"

Jenny laughed and at the same time went pink.

"Lots of unmarried girls have eaten a gingerbread man and hoped something good will happen!"

"Then maybe I'd better give it a try!" said Jenny.

They cleared up and Selina as a treat reached her best china tea set out of a cupboard and brewed a pot of tea. "I think we bakers deserve a little gingerbread ourselves. Just to make sure it's good."

Jenny grinned. Dear Selina. How she admired her. She knew that the little woman had been cooking meals for the Biddalls since she was thirteen years old. Just imagine!

The gingerbread was delicious. Jenny licked her fingers. She wrapped up the little gingerbread man and put him in a pocket. She still hadn't asked about a lift to Carlisle. Now that she felt calmer she wasn't quite sure what to think.

32

Battle In The Square

The final day, Monday. The Ghost Show opened up peacefully enough in the Market Square in Cleator Moor, a small mining town. An afternoon rush of townsfolk and children began and all was well until the evening when the mood began to change.

Flaring lights hissed over the stalls as a crowd of miners and their girls came surging in. Heavy, tough looking men, the salt of the earth, declared Rudge, who was pretty tough himself. Many of the miners were Irish and glad of the prospect of plenty of work, for the town straddled good mining country, red iron ore, and rich black coal.

Jenny, despite wanting to stay clear of Henry, found it was impossible to avoid him. Selina with an almost knowing smile had asked her to keep him well supplied with gingerbread. Whether she liked it or not, Jenny found she was having to work alongside him. Even so, she spoke only when she had to.

Uncle Victor drew them aside. "Stay close to the theatre," he urged. "Don't wander about in the town."

They were surprised.

"Something's brewing," said Victor ominously. "And warn young Snivel, just in case."

"In case what?" asked Henry, but Victor was off to the Aunt Sally alongside to see old Mr Lodge.

Jenny said: "What's the matter?"

"We'd better do as he says and stay here in the theatre. You had anyway."

Jenny was indignant. "I can go anywhere I want, thank you! I don't need your permission."

"But he says stay in. I've got to go out and fetch the gingerbread from Selina."

"Well I've got to fetch it too. And I baked it! I'll go now."

"Wait!"

Why didn't she listen?

Jenny flounced off. Henry! Always giving orders. She passed the entrance. Whatever had Victor been talking about? She liked Cleator Moor.

Snivel went to the front entrance as she left to take a look for himself. A crowd had gathered and he had a strange feeling he was being watched. He went back to tell Henry.

Henry half listened, still upset about Jenny.

"It's nowt. Folk is allus looking."

Snivel knew he hadn't explained it very well.

Jenny collected a box of gingerbread from Selina and got back to the edge of the square. A group of men was shouting angrily at one another. She paused, wondering how to get round and was still undecided when the nearest man hit his neighbour in the face. At once others began to join in.

Jenny clutched the box. Her heart pounding, she pushed past in a panic, fearful she would get caught in the tussle. Not until she was inside the theatre did she begin to feel safe.

"What's the matter?" said Henry.

"Nothing! Here's the gingerbread."

Boos and jeers sounded outside. The fighting seemed to be spreading.

"They'll soon stop. They'll not bother us," said Henry.

Zella appeared. "Are you all right?" she asked. She sounded worried. "A miner's been attacked, in a pub. Someone hit him with a spike or something. Some louts have been trying to get off with the miners' girls."

"What about the Ghost Show? When are we going to start?"

"George says we must wait. He says it's too dangerous. But I'd better get back."

Eight o'clock. The sound of fighting was getting louder.

Backstage, Henry sorted the gingerbread onto a tray as Jenny sat disconsolately on a box. Neither of them spoke. Everything seemed to be turning sour. Selina had told her how Henry and Snivel had had a bad time when some things were stolen. Then there had been Zella, and now, their final night, everything was turning into a brawl.

A crash of splintering wood made them jump with fright. The ground shook as something heavy crashed outside the canvas walls.

Henry thrust the gingerbread tray into her hands. "Hold onto this!"

Through the side exit he came to a shocked halt. A brawling gang of men confronted him. Behind them Mr Lodge's Aunt Sally lay in ruins.

He yelled: "Snivel! Old Mr Lodge, he could be under that lot!"

"Crikey. He'll be dead!"

Ignoring the fighting, they dragged at the tangled canvas and struts. Henry was shouting: "Mr Lodge! Mr Lodge!"

There was no sign of the old man.

"He ain't here," cried Snivel.

Not until they were pulling apart the worst of the wreckage did they hear a faint croaky voice.

Henry yelled: "Mr Lodge! It's Snivel and me."

The old man's grey head showed through a gap.

"Young Henry? Get me out."

They pulled the mess apart and helped the showman to his feet.

Fresh booing filled the square.

"Perishing louts!"

"Easy now," said Henry gently. He picked up the old man's spectacles and bent them straight. "Can you walk all right?"

"Try stopping me." Mr Lodge was limping and his face had been grazed.

Between them they got to his caravan. "I'll just rest a bit. But the prizes . . ."

"We'll get 'em," said Henry.

They hurried back.

They were gathering up scattered dolls as a crash of breaking glass made them halt.

"Someone else has copped it."

And then: "Crikey! It's the Ghost Show."

They dumped the dolls under the canvas and ran to the front entrance. But they were not the first there. A phantom figure in white raced in ahead of them.

33

Two Heroines

Jenny waited anxiously on her own. The sound of fighting was getting louder. She was tempted to look out to see what was happening when a tearing noise came from close behind. To her horror a long knife blade was sticking through the canvas. She turned cold with terror.

The knife started to slice downwards.

Jenny's mind raced. If she called out who would hear? The theatre was empty. Hardly daring to breathe she got behind a packing case as a man's head and shoulders came pushing through the slit. A moment later he climbed inside. Unaware of her presence, he hurried up the aisle.

Her heart pounding, Jenny was about to look up into the theatre as a crash of glass sounded. Moments later the man came running down the aisle. He was clutching a long black box. Jenny trembled. He was stealing the cashbox!

Desperate, she could think of only one way to stop him. The thief was pushing the box through the slit as she brought the gingerbread tray crashing down on his head. The blow knocked him to the floor. Wildly she grabbed at him round his neck.

The man was small but he was strong. He hit out viciously, punching her in the ribs. She gasped with pain as he struggled to get to his feet, and moments later he would have broken free had help not arrived. A figure came down the aisle at a run, doubled up and in a brilliant acrobatic leap landed feet first in the man's back, knocking him flat.

It was Zella!

They yelled for help and were fighting to hold him when Henry ran in with George and Rudge. Between them they pinned the man down.

George saw the slit in the canvas and looked angry. He shook the man hard.

"Leggo! That's my arm!"

"Your arm?" growled George. "You're lucky it's not your neck!"

Other folk arrived.

Snivel bobbed up and down excitedly. "I know him! It's the bloke from the rat tub. I knew he was a thief!"

George tied the man's hands behind him and gave the knots an extra tug. "Thank you – everyone. Thank you. You've just saved the day's takings."

"It was the girls who stopped him," said Henry loyally.

Jenny looked at Zella. Zella looked at Jenny.

"You arrived just in time," said Jenny.

"I didn't know you could wrestle," said Zella.

For the first time they smiled at one another.

Both had suffered several punches. Zella had escaped serious injury but a trickle of blood ran down Jenny's face from a cut.

George said: "Rudge, take this villain to your van, and keep him tied up. I'll deal with him later."

Henry tugged a piece of cloth from a pocket, made sure it looked clean, and shyly approached Jenny. "Here," he said softly, "let me look at that."

She was still shaking as she let him dab her cheek.

"It's not too bad, but it needs cleaning with antiseptic."

Selina said: "Henry's right. Come with me, Jenny, to our van."

Jenny nodded. Her whole body seemed to be aching. She turned to go, then paused. She touched Henry gently on the hand.

"Thanks," she whispered.

"You were really brave," he told her.

Outside, police whistles blasted the night. The Biddalls hurried out to look.

The fair was full of brawling men. A burly sergeant and three constables had arrived and came pushing through the battling crowd, their capes flung back. Somehow they reached the heart of the struggle, fending off would-be attackers with truncheons, and finally reaching their targets.

Booing filled the square. Courageously the policemen began dragging men apart. Others paused to look, and momentarily there was a lull.

"Keep on fighting, lads," yelled the sergeant hoarsely, "and you'll land in clink! All of you. But stop right now and we might all get home for our suppers!"

It could easily not have worked. But to the sergeant's voice another was added, strong and helpful.

"Roll up! Roll up! For a Ghost Show special!"

It was George. Jacketless, in cycle breeches and shirtsleeves he stepped boldly to the front of the theatre booth calling through a megaphone.

"Tonight! Open house at the Ghost Show! Come and see the Ghost Show free! For nothing! Everyone invited! Especially the miners!"

Henry and Snivel goggled in admiration. The showman looked so strong and reassuring. Henry wished more than anything that he could be just like him.

"Give us ten minutes to pull out the splinters," yelled George, "and we'll show you the best ghosts Cleator Moor has ever seen!"

It worked. They were listening! A cheer rang out.

With perfect timing Joey bobbed up on his giant clown boots. He waved a hideous yellow skull. "Don't be scared, lads! Ten minutes and we'll give you the fright of your life!"

And suddenly the tension evaporated; the fighting ended. Men grinned. They nursed black eyes, they began swapping yarns. A group of miners hesitated, then went across and helped to get the Aunt Sally the right way up. The battle of Cleator Moor was over.

"Wow!" said Henry.

"Yeah!" said Snivel.

They went back to collect up the dolls. "Let's go and tell Mr Lodge."

The old man was in his caravan waiting for them. His face was bruised and his jacket torn but he looked calm, and it was obvious he had something on his mind.

34

Mr Lodge's Big Idea

They dumped a heap of dolls on a bunk.

"Good lads! You got 'em."

He laughed. "Sit down. Sit down. You're two good 'uns, you are. I've been wanting to talk to you."

But Henry was dying to tell him the news. "Guess what! The girls have caught a thief pinching the cashbox."

"A thief?"

Henry described how Jenny and Zella had grabbed the man, and how George was about to do a special show just for the miners, and it was starting soon.

Mr. Lodge shifted the dolls along the bunk. "Goodness. Then I must be quick."

His face became intent. "I've been thinking about what you said, how you want to go places, and see things. But are you serious? I mean, really serious?"

Henry's face lit up. "Sniv and me's talked a lot. But we can't do owt, not yet."

"We gotta get us jobs," said Snivel.

"Of course. And that's what I'm on about."

Henry hesitated. He didn't want to offend the old man. "It's not puppets we are thinking of, I mean.

Mr Lodge smiled. "Of course not. What you want is something up to date. And I think I know exactly what."

Mr Lodge was coming to his big idea.

"I've thought a lot about this. What would you say to starting your own show? Going round the fairs, like everyone, like George does with the ghosts?"

Henry grinned thinking the old man was kidding.

But no, Mr Lodge went on: "Of course you'll need something new . . . really new, something people will come rushing to see. And I think I know the very thing."

Henry and Snivel glanced at one another, puzzled. What was the old man on about?

The showman spread a paper on the table before them.

"What you want is something that's just been invented. You want living pictures."

Both lads looked blank.

Mr Lodge shifted the page round so they could read the title. It was the showmen's trade paper *The Era* and full of fairground news.

"Everyone's excited about 'em. Show folk is anyway. Pictures that walk just like they was real people!"

Henry blinked, puzzled. "Walk? How can they? Pictures can't move."

"You have me there," Mr Lodge confessed. "I don't know how it's done, but George has talked about it."

"They must be lantern slides," said Snivel.

"No, lantern slides get pushed about. Lantern slides do just that, slide. But living pictures . . . they move by themselves, like they was magic. Like they is real."

Henry tried to grasp the idea. It didn't sound possible.

"Albert calls 'em filums. He's really excited. He's seen one that's full of soldiers. Lines and lines of 'em. They come marching past you as real as anything! Like they was going off to war. And all of 'em tramping along as if they was outside here in the street!

"But there's another, a train. It comes rolling straight at you like it's going to run you down! Albert says it's real frightening. But the train never hits you."

Henry and Snivel listened open mouthed.

"Why not?"

Mr Lodge shook his head. "Cause it's not a real train. It's a picture. Like it's living. One that moves."

He turned the pages of *The Era* to a big advertisement. "Look." It showed a man turning a handle on a magic lantern.

"But that's nobbut a drawing," objected Henry. "A lantern."

"Yes," said Mr Lodge, "but the real thing isn't. And it's not a lantern; it's a projector. Everyone's getting very excited.

"What's important, a projector's going to be demonstrated very soon up here in the North. At Newcastle for one place, and at Kendal for another.

"Now Kendal I'd say is real handy."

He flattened the magazine. "You wind round the handle and it sends filum through it with lots of little pictures all moving."

Henry still found it hard to believe.

The old man turned the page to another advert. "There's even a projector for sale, right now. Down in London."

Henry gaped. He read the price. Twenty-two pounds!

"Of course it needs filums as well. Albert's been and talked to men who stand outside selling 'em. They cut lengths of filum off a long roll and charge so many pennies a foot."

"Here in Cumberland?"

"No, no. Down in Soho, a place in London. They just stand in the street and cut off long bits of it. Maybe they'll do it in Newcastle too. But wait . . ."

He adjusted his glasses and stared at the magazine. "Yes. Bless us, the Kendal one's this Friday! Grand Cinematograph Demonstration. Kendal Town Hall."

Henry was becoming interested. Living pictures! How could pictures live? It did not seem possible, yet Mr Lodge was deadly serious. Even so, a projector thing . . . it would take years to save twenty-two pounds. Tomorrow he and Snivel wouldn't even have jobs. The ghosts would be off to Scotland without them.

A voice sounded outside. Joey was calling.

"They're going to start!" warned Snivel.

Henry got to his feet, his head buzzing with ideas.

"We'll need to finish our talk later," said Mr Lodge.

35

A Night To Remember

A final performance! George was as good as his word, the Ghost Show reopened to a fanfare of trumpeting.

Joey emerged at the front of the booth, bright and breezy. "La-dies and genn-el-men!" he bellowed. A sea of miners' faces turned towards him. "Step up! Step up! A special ghost show! FREE! Come and be frighted!"

The theatre filled up in moments. What a clamour! How the ghostly shrieks sounded. How the miners roared in approval. Never had the Biddalls worked so hard.

The performance ended amid loud enthusiastic applause. George, tired, smiling with satisfaction, moved to the front of the crowded benches and thanked the audience for being such good sports. No audience could have been better.

"God bless the miners!" he called. "Be sure we'll come back to Cleator Moor!"

He stepped away to lusty cheering and Henry felt a lump come into his throat. It was a night they would all remember.

The weary Biddalls gathered backstage.

"Well done everyone!" George told them. "We'll close the front for now and clear up in the morning. First, though, the prisoner. Have you got him, Rudge?"

Faces became grim. Yet everyone knew it had to be done.

Rudge went to the lock-up caravan and led the man back. His hands were untied and his shabby coat removed. He looked scared.

George stood over the prisoner. "Just do it."

Henry and Jenny pushed through. The man was kneeling in front of the slit canvas. The showmen and women watched him struggle to sew it up.

"Make a good job of it," ordered George sternly, "or we'll make you undo it and do it again."

The man was sweating. His hands, so swift to slip into people's pockets, seemed clumsy when it came to using a wax thread and a sail maker's needle. But the showman was unrelenting. Not until the last stitch had been done and the slit examined did George allow the man to get to his feet.

"Young Snivel, have you got the man's coat? Heavy is it? Let me look."

The showman felt at an inside pocket. "I might have known!" He held up a watch, and then he found a whole string of them.

"Someone's going to be mighty glad to see this lot. But what's this? Well, I'm blessed!"

George pulled out a long green object. It was heavy with money.

"The purse! And see!"

He held up a tiny silver Christening spoon and, to Jenny's delight, her missing train tickets.

"Quite a haul!" exclaimed George.

Henry and Snivel stared excitedly at one another. So that's what had happened!

George turned to them. "I think we all owe you an apology me lads . . . me especially!"

"Nay," began Henry, wanting to say it didn't matter, but he was interrupted as Joey arrived with a policeman.

George turned to the officer: "Constable, this man is all yours! And a few trinkets to go with him."

The thief was hauled away.

"Lads, we are very sorry," said George. "We should have known all along you wouldn't do anything to let us down."

Loud clapping broke out.

Henry and Snivel grinned happily.

Jenny glanced at Zella and they smiled. Justice had been done. More than that, the missing money had been found.

The Market Square stood silent at last. Everyone was off to bed.

Outside, Jenny paused. "Henry, I shouldn't have said like I did."

"Nay." He shook his head. "It's all my fault." He hesitated: "Shall I see you tomorrow?"

"If you want."

His heart leapt. He almost went on to ask were they friends again, but he thought better of it. Better not rush things.

In the last caravan down the line Snivel was all keyed up.

"Hey, are ya there?" He peered down from his bunk as Henry collapsed in a tired heap. "I've got summat. Summat important."

Henry groaned. "Tell us tomorrow. Douse the lamp and get to sleep."

"No, you gotta see now! I pinched it out of the coat."

That made Henry sit up.

Snivel handed him a small round object.

Henry's eyes widened. "My watch? How'd you get it?"

"Easy," said Snivel. "It was in with the rest."

"Crikey. Wow, thanks. I thought I'd lost it for good."

Snivel grinned.

"There's summat else . . . that glass thing. The statue. I wasn't going to pinch it ya know. I was only looking. But Joey, he come in and I bunged it under his mattress."

"Didn't he see you?"

"No. He come in that quick."

Henry said: "Get to sleep."

But Snivel went on: "You knew it was me all along, din't ya?"

"Did I?" said Henry. "No I didn't," he lied.

He sank into the covers. What a week. And now it was almost over. Well, come the morning it would be. He put the watch next to him on his pillow and lay listening to it ticking. He was going to miss the Biddalls. He was going to miss the Ghost Show.

36

The Best Show That Ever Was

Hammering woke Henry and Snivel long before breakfast on Tuesday. They hurried out to find Joey doing his best to help Mr Lodge repair his stall. Soon everyone would be leaving. Despite the lateness of the night before no one seemed tired. Henry was pleased when Jenny came out to help.

She had gone to bed with mixed feelings about Henry, and she couldn't help feeling jealous of Zella, though that seemed best forgotten now. Jenny was well aware that in the past she had kissed a couple of boys herself. And she had to admit she cared quite a bit about Henry, most of the time anyway.

With five at work they made good progress, nailing up the framework and stitching on canvas patches. An hour later the Aunt Sally was in working order and being packed up.

"It got a bit exciting last night!" said Mr Lodge.

Henry grinned. "I thought we were in for a fight."

Mr Lodge felt for his keys. "Now, I'd better lock up."

"I'll carry the tools."

The old man and Henry went together.

"Handy Henry, eh?"

Henry grinned. "Sort of. One of mum's jokes."

The old showman gave him a questioning glance. "Have you been thinking about my idea? About getting your own show?"

Henry nodded that he had. "Them living picture things. I've been thinking about them a lot."

Mr Lodge nodded approvingly. "Come on, we must eat or Selina will be telling us off for being late. We'll talk later."

The Biddall's caravan was overflowing.

Somehow it wasn't breakfast and somehow it wasn't lunch.

"Any more sausages?"

"Tea. More tea!"

"And jelly, more jelly, please."

"Not jelly with sausages?"

"Yeah. Well, sort of, no, oh well, all right."

"Be sure everything is eaten," warned Selina.

They did, getting up their strength for the journey ahead. An hour to go and the Biddalls would leave little Cleator Moor and head off north up to Annan, all set to frighten the Scots.

But it was a sad time, too. Jenny, Henry and Snivel planned to travel with them only as far as Whitehaven, and once there they would catch the Keswick train. Their days with the Ghost Show were almost over.

George smiled hugely at the head of the table and raised his cup. "I know this is only tea, and not really strong enough . . ."

"Pardon me," corrected Selina. "I put a dash of rum in yours."

"Oh, did you? Well thank you for that, my love. You all know what I mean. Quiet please! I want to propose a toast of thanks to our young helpers, Henry and Snivel. They've worked as hard as any of us – and no showmen can say better than that. We are going to miss them."

"To Henry and Snivel. Here! Here!"

"As to the young ladies . . ." George paused and nodded approvingly. "Don't let anyone step out of line or you'll find yourself arrested by two of the prettiest constables you'll ever hope to meet!"

Laughter filled the caravan. Jenny and Zella had plenty of bruises and Jenny had the cut to her face. Zella's angel face was uninjured. Both girls knew they had been lucky to escape real injury.

"To Jenny and Zella!"

Jenny blushed. Zella smiled demurely, being well used to compliments.

And then quite suddenly it was Henry who had everyone's attention. Really he had planned no such thing, but now he held up his tea mug and everyone fell silent.

"I j-just want to say, that is . . . Well here's t-to the best Ghost Show that ever was! I mean . . ."

He paused and felt the words sticking. He caught a smile of encouragement from Jenny.

"Well, we just know that no one could have been kinder to us than all of you. Not anyone, not anywhere."

"God bless you, young sir. Thank you. To the Ghost Show!"

"Bravo!"

"Till we all meet again," called Uncle Victor.

"Yeah," said Snivel.

Henry sat down. It was strange but he was feeling both happy and sad at the same time.

The meal over, Mr Lodge signalled Henry to one side.

"So what about Kendal?" he asked. "You're thinking of going on Friday, that is."

Henry was surprised. "Who told you?"

Mr Lodge smiled. "No one. People think old men are sitting fast asleep, but we're not you know. Not always."

Henry said: "We thought we'd try, Snivel and me, to see the filums. We want to go and look."

The old man shook his head. "No, no, that's no good! You've got to get started! You've got to get a projector.

"See . . ."

He pulled something out of his jacket. "I've been thinking about this for a while. This is just between you and me. It's only a loan."

He handed an envelope to Henry.

"Go on, take a look."

Henry's mouth opened. The envelope was bulging with a wodge of pound notes.

"I can't," he said.

"Take it. Take it. You'll be able to get going. But remember it's only a loan, till you get earning. You can't set up a filum show without money."

"But you hardly know us."

"I know you well enough," said Mr Lodge. His faded eyes lit up. "You can't know the pleasure it gives me to see young people starting out in life.

"Now, no more! I must finish packing or the rest will be leaving before I'm ready."

Bursting with news, Henry found the others.

"*How much?*" said Jenny, astounded.

"Twenty-five," said Henry. "Twenty-five pounds."

He opened the envelope and showed them the notes. They were crumpled, but they were real enough.

Jenny didn't really understand.

Snivel goggled. "Crikey! He must nutty."

"But what's it for?" asked Jenny.

"It's for our own show! Travelling, like George does."

Jenny was open-mouthed.

"A Ghost Show?"

"No, no!" Henry's face filled with delight. "Nothing like it! It's something modern. Living Pictures. Pictures that move and walk about by themselves!"

Jenny almost laughed. She had never heard of such a thing.

Henry was suddenly sure. "We'll do it together. You and me and Snivel! We'll make our fortune!"

"Me?"

Their own show? How could they? Not just like that. Well, Zella obviously did, but that was different.

Snivel licked his lips. "Hey, if we're going to be a proper business I want my proper name: Frederick."

Henry grinned. "Freddy it is! Seriously, Mr Lodge has only lent us the money. But if we find a proper projector we can buy it right away. And filums, and everything."

Snivel looked worried. "What if it don't work? How'll we pay him?"

Henry talked quickly, suddenly sure. "We'll do lots of shows. We'll get the money like that! We'll need a tent . . . and a cart and horse."

"Oh, there's my Bellow," Jenny said excitedly. "My pony, he's at Fingland."

Henry was about to say they might need something a bit younger than her old pony but he didn't. One thing at a time. First they must buy a projector.

Though outwardly he remained calm Henry's senses were racing. Their own show! A showman. He wanted that more than anything. He hugged himself with excitement. Suddenly everything began to seem possible.

They must get to Kendal by Friday.

37

How The Angel Flew

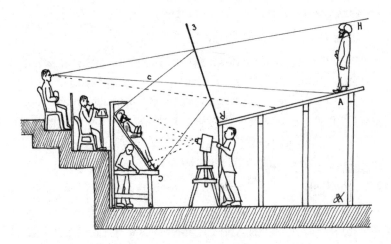

The train rattled along beside Bassenthwaite, smoke trailing out across the lake. Whitehaven lay far behind and Keswick was just four more miles to go.

There was something Jenny longed to find out.

"You've got to tell me, how does she do it? I mean, Zella – how does she fly?"

Henry had worked it out at last. "It's that big sheet of glass across the front of the stage."

"I've seen it," said Snivel. 'It's a whopper."

"It's fourteen feet right across, and the glass leans forward, towards the seats so the audience can't see it. People look straight through it and don't know it's there."

He drew it on paper. "Secretly some of the actors dress up like ghosts and hide under the stage. A light shines on them and a mirror reflects their pictures up onto the glass on the stage. What you see is the actors' reflections on the glass. Other actors really are on the stage and the ghosts seem to be next to them."

"But Zella, how does she fly?"

"She lies on a trolley down below. The front of the stage hides her from the audience. Someone winds a handle and pulls her along. She isn't flying, not really, it only seems she is. As she's pulled along her picture's reflected onto the glass up above. The audience just sees her white reflection moving!"

"Nay," said Snivel. "I've never seen no trolley."

It had taken Henry longer to figure that out.

"You won't because the trolley's covered in black cloth. The black doesn't show on the glass above. Only Zella's reflection shows 'cause she's dressed in white. It's real clever."

"It's real spooky," said Snivel.

"Hey up, here's Keswick!"

The train was gliding in alongside a platform.

Snivel went to unload Henry's bike.

"Are we really going to get our own film thing?" said Jenny.

"Yes, but we haven't much time."

The Kendal film demonstration was only three days away.

Jenny didn't like to voice her doubts. "I bet people say we're too young to have our own show."

"Let 'em," said Henry. "Look at Zella. She's only fifteen."

"She's different."

"I don't see how. I'm nearly seventeen. I'll grow a moustache and look older if I have to."

Jenny laughed. She hugged his arm. He had changed. Somehow he was more self-assured.

Henry hitched his trousers. "First we must get to Fingland to see my mum."

"I know what we'll do." Jenny spoke crisply. "We'll go to Mr Benk's, the carrier. He brought me to Keswick."

"He'll charge us."

"Yes, but not a lot. What day is it? Tuesday? We get deliveries at Fingland, at Aunt May's on Wednesday, tomorrow. Let's go to his house now. And if he can't take us then we'll get someone else."

Henry grinned at the budding manager.

Mr Benk was in and yes he was going up Carlisle way tomorrow. His Wednesday run. For a fee, of course. Fingland, eh? The bike a bit extra. Two bikes? What other bike? A butcher's bike? In a field? Well, yes, but that would cost more, paid in advance.

They split up. Jenny set off to surprise her cousin, and Henry went to Snivel's home.

The moment Snivel stepped inside his dad whacked him on the head with a slipper.

"Stole his bike, you blithering idiot!" Bob Earnshaw was crimson. "I'll brain you! Old Potter was upstairs. He saw you take it! Raging mad he was! He was going for the police if Sadie hadn't stepped in!"

Sadie it emerged had hurried to see Mr Potter and as a peace offering had taken him a meat and potato pie (their own supper). She promised absolutely that Snivel would get the bike back, and it was kind of Mr Potter to be so understanding and it was good to have such a good neighbour and she'd collect the empty pie dish in the morning.

Sadie fed them sausages and mash, casting a knowing grimace at Snivel.

But matters calmed and the lads poured out their adventures to the astonished listeners. Nothing was said about the precious £25 or anything about film shows.

38

A Time To Be Bold

Three days later Henry and Snivel came to a stop on the pavement outside Kendal's looming Town Hall. It was mid-morning and the town centre was full of people shopping.

"This looks like it."

"Nay, I dunno." Snivel looked doubtful. "There's no notice or owt."

The building seemed so solid, monumental, overpowering.

They had been travelling most of the night and now that they had arrived Snivel was feeling nervous.

"You go in and I'll hang about."

But Henry shook his head. "Better if we all know what to do."

Snivel looked unhappy. His left boot was troubling him. It was coming apart and was starting to flap as he walked. "Nay, I'll stop out. It's Jenny as ought ta be 'ere."

She had stayed behind at Fingland to help her Aunt May.

A lot had happened. On Wednesday Mr Benk had carried the three of them by cart from Keswick to Fingland and during supper they had poured out their adventures to Henry's mother and Jenny's Aunt May.

They couldn't have had a more surprised audience.

They stayed at Fingland all Thursday and it was long after midnight before Henry and Snivel set off to walk eight windy miles to Carlisle and catch a train south. Everything now depended on what happened in Kendal.

"Let's go in," said Henry.

He felt scruffy and not at all like someone who had £25 safely hidden in a money pouch. But they had come all this way and now it was time to be bold.

Inside they were cheered by the sight of a large billboard.

TODAY!

Grand Cinematograph Exposition!!!

The Renowned

Mr Algernon Sharples will demonstrate

The Amazing! The Magical!

LIVING Pictures!

They walk! They run!

Don't miss an Astounding

Modern Miracle!

A Scientific Wonder!!!

It was the right place. It was the right day. This was what they had come to see.

It was as far as they got.

"And where do you think you're going?"

A uniformed attendant eyed Snivel's flapping boot.

"We've come in to see the films," said Henry.

"Filums? Oh, no you haven't! You can clear off."

Snivel came to the rescue. He sat on the floor and started to take off the troublesome boot.

"What the devil do you think you're doing?" cried the man. He grabbed at the titch. "Get out!"

Snivel yelled, and then to make sure, he did some extra yells.

Good old Snivel! Henry's feelings swung from frustration to hope. He slipped into the Town Hall.

39

An Amazing Machine

The exhibition room was crowded and Henry moved quickly to a seat, his face bright with excitement. A projector was standing in the middle of the room pointing at a white sheet pinned to a wall.

People were talking in hushed tones and looking around expectantly. Gradually, however, it become apparent that something was wrong. An elegant man in a dark suit and a high-standing wing-collar was in the middle of a cluster of people by the projector. He seemed to be arguing.

"Is this seat taken?"

Henry moved aside to let a man sit down. The newcomer hooked a walking stick over the back of a chair.

"Here to see the living pictures are you?"

"Business," said Henry cautiously. He glanced at the stranger. His face was weather-beaten and he wore a large nebbed cap.

"Seems there's a hold up."

The stranger's next remark took him by surprise.

"You wouldn't be Henry would you?"

Henry stared warily. It was no one he knew.

"Yes, but who said?"

"I'm Albert, Albert Biddall. George is my father. I got a message from Victor. He said to look out for you."

The showman laughed at Henry's astonished expression.

"He thought you might like a bit of help. I mean if you want to buy a projector."

Good old Uncle Victor!

"Yes, I do! We want to get our own show, me and me pals."

Albert Biddall sat forward. "Look's like something's happening."

The wing-collar man had moved to the front of the audience and was announcing that he was extremely sorry about the delay, and that he was Mr Sharples, and the projector had arrived safely – everyone could see it had. A splendid, in fact an amazing machine, an Eragraph. But alas, the films had not arrived. They were coming by train and unfortunately would not reach Kendal until the afternoon, or possibly tomorrow morning.

Groans filled the room.

Mr Sharples went on hurriedly to say that once the films had arrived . . .

He was still speaking as people began to rise from their seats.

"That's bad news!" said Albert. He reached for his stick. "Come on, let's see if we can sort this out."

Henry whispered: "Is the projector no good?"

"Good? They're brilliant. They're calling it an Eragraph. Fact is . . . " He hesitated. "I've just ordered one in London for myself!"

"Crikey!" Henry was impressed.

Albert pushed his way forward and addressed the winged-collared man. "Hello? Can we have a look? My friend is very interested."

Mr Sharples' face lit up. "Certainly! A pleasure." The man's gloom lifted. Enthusiastically he produced a short length of film.

"I've only this bit of film with me. A test piece. It's just long enough for lacing up, but I can show you that much."

Henry got up close and was thrilled. The projector was fastened to a wooden board. A small chimney rose from a squat lantern house at the back; but the best bits were the gears and the cranking handle, with a shiny lens fixed in front.

The salesman threaded the test strip, and showed how to focus the picture.

"Once you begin projecting, it's important to turn the handle smoothly."

He cranked the handle and the strip of film swiftly fed through. It tumbled out at the bottom into a black bag.

"A perfect machine!" He rescued the film. "At £22, not cheap, I know, but amazing! Films, of course, cost extra, five pence a foot."

Henry was catching Mr Sharples' enthusiasm. He examined the test strip. It seemed quite long and had sprocket holes. The last few feet were full of tiny pictures showing a man standing.

"Won't this piece work now?"

Mr Sharples grimaced. "Yes and no. It needs a long length to show it properly. But it would work, though briefly of course."

"Please, couldn't we try?" begged Henry, desperate to see even a bit of the film projected.

Mr Sharples did not look over happy, but he was a salesman and keen not to miss a sale. He looked at Albert. "You realise it would show on-screen only for seconds, but if you really want to try, you need to practice cranking the handle first."

"No, no." Albert smiled. "Let Henry try."

Mr Sharples eyed Henry's worn clothes but if he were surprised he made no comment. "Certainly. Perhaps the young sir would care to stand alongside and take hold?"

Henry did as he said. Excited, he grasped the projector handle.

"Whatever you do, you must not rush it," warned Mr Sharples. "Off you go."

Nervously Henry began to turn the handle. It took several moments to settle to a smooth rhythm.

"Good! Very good. Stop and I'll load the film. In fact you can do it!"

Guided by Mr Sharples, Henry threaded the short test film through the machine. The first few feet were blank and then came the short length of tiny pictures.

"I'll light the gas jets so we can heat the lime," said Mr Sharples. He pointed at a metal filter. "That's the dowser to stop the film burning. Raise it the moment you start, but be careful. It can be dangerous."

Henry waited excitedly.

Mr Sharples produced a box and placed a white cone of lime onto a burner. Taps were connected to two bottles.

"Two gasses," explained Mr. Sharples. "Hydrogen and oxygen." He struck a match and turned a tap. The gas hissed and burst into flame. "Hydrogen! Now see when we add oxygen."

The flame was heating the lime as Mr Sharples turned on the oxygen. A brilliant ray of limelight lanced out and filled the screen.

"Raise the filter!" cried Mr Sharples urgently. "And turn!"

Henry obeyed.

The film whirred through the machine. Henry gasped. A picture of a gardener filled the screen. The man was staring into a hosepipe nozzle. Then the screen turned white again as the film vanished into the black bag.

"Wow!" Henry was open-mouthed. "He moved!"

There was no doubt about it, the man had been moving.

Everyone started speaking at once. Henry was caught up in the excitement. Their own show! Could it really happen? He was beginning to see it might.

"But how does it work?" he asked.

Mr Sharples held up the strip of film so they could see the tiny pictures.

"It's like this! Pretend you are looking at a closed hand. The next picture shows the hand has opened a bit. And the next one it's opened a little bit more, and so on. Lots more pictures go on showing it opening and in the last one it's fully open. Up to 24 of these little pictures (frames they call 'em) are projected onto the screen every second . . . too fast for our eyes to tell we're seeing lots of separate pictures. Magically, the images seem to merge and the hand looks as if it's moving."

"I want to buy one!" said Henry, his face bright. "A projector, I mean! And lots . . . " He made sure he said it properly: "Lots of films!"

Startled, the salesman glanced at Albert, and then at Henry. "And how would sir be wanting to pay?" he asked patronisingly.

"Cash!" replied Henry. His voice rang with confidence. He pulled out the envelope, fat with money. At once the salesman's attitude altered. Respectfully he acknowledged Henry's order.

Henry counted out the notes and Albert arranged for a new Eragraph to be delivered to Henry's mother at Fingland along with a selection of films. Mr Sharples wrote a receipt and Albert witnessed it.

Mr Sharples said: "An exciting time lies ahead of you young sir."

"You can say that again," said Albert. He laughed. "From now on you're going to be a joiner, painter, advertiser, tea maker, labourer, in fact a Jack of all Trades! Now let's go and get some breakfast."

"Oh help, I must find Snivel, me pal – I mean, Freddy."

They left the Town Hall. "We'll have to get a tent," said Henry. "And a cart – and everything."

"If I was you," suggested Albert. "I'd fix up a trial show first. Get used to it before you set out properly on the road. There's a fair coming up at Penrith. Get yourself a start there."

Henry gulped excitedly. He would. That's exactly what he would do! "And George . . . Mr Biddall? Films?"

Albert became more serious. "Ghosts are great, but living pictures are going to change the world."

"But the Ghost Show?"

"It'll keep going a good while yet." He smiled wryly. "Ghosts have a habit of appearing unexpectedly. And George is trying them both – living pictures and ghosts! I reckon there's room on the road for all of us."

Henry set out to find Snivel. A lot now had to happen.

40

Even Their Mouths Moved

Penrith's Market Square resounded with booming organ music. People were crowding into the fair as a glittering merry-go-round struck up a noisy welcome. It wasn't the only barrel organ sounding out, but it was the loudest. The crowd didn't yet know it, but today something surprising was going to happen in the town. Amid the mass of fairground sideshows and stalls something totally new had arrived, something as yet hardly understood – a Film Tent.

Curious, passers-by paused to read the notice board:

LIVING PICTURES!

A modern miracle

AMAZING

pictures

They Walk!

They Run and Jump!

Adults 1d

Children ONLY a ha-penny!

We start at

12 NOON!

But all was not well. Noon had passed and the tent flaps remained closed.

Inside, Jenny was in tears. "What are we going to do?"

Until now everything had seemed fine. They arranged to have the projector and films delivered to Penrith. Jenny's Aunt May had lent them a small cart and had even found an old agricultural show-tent up in the loft. It was small but would just about do. Loaded up, they had set out with Jenny's pony, Bellow.

After a long trek they had arrived in Penrith Market Square. Hurriedly they found a pitch and set up their tent between the merry-go-round and the Fat Lady's booth.

Next a race up to the station to collect a wooden crate and then back down through the town to the square.

Tense with excitement, Henry broke open the lid and pulled out the packing.

"Gosh!"

The shining projector took away his breath. He ran his fingers over the gears.

"It's going to be really good."

But there was a problem. Snivel looked through the crate.

"There's no filum!"

"What!"

They searched through the packaging. There was only the projector.

Henry was appalled. People could be heard waiting outside the tent talking. He saw only one option.

"Bring in the board. We can't do the show."

"Wait a minute," said Jenny, ever practical. "Where's the delivery note?" She got it from the box and straightened out the creases. "Henry! Look! It says two boxes, not one!"

Henry ran all the way to the station.

The porter was apologetic. "Here is it: Master Henry Hodgekin. Urgent."

He handed over a cardboard box. "Got put on the wrong shelf."

Henry ran all the way back.

They were very late.

"We gotta start right away," he ordered.

Snivel was alarmed. "But we hasn't seen the filums! We can't show 'em without seeing 'em first!"

"We're going to have to!" said Henry. "We're running too far behind."

He mounted the projector on the crate while Jenny tore open the cardboard box. Inside was a black film sack. Neatly coiled with it was the precious film.

Henry held the roll to the light. He could just make out the first of the tiny pictures.

"Sniv, go out and tell folk we're going to start in a few minutes!"

He laced the film through the projector.

"The sack, we need the sack!"

Jenny hooked it on under the projector stand, ready to catch the film.

"Let's get going."

"No, wait." Jenny paused. She turned her hair up onto the back of her head and fastened it into a silky bun. It was time she looked a bit older.

Henry grinned.

"Now!" He called: "Sniv, we're ready! Tell 'em we're starting! And say films, not filums."

Jenny took charge of the entrance. Their first show! Full of excitement, she opened the flap and nodded to Snivel to start calling.

Snivel hadn't rehearsed what he was going to say but he had often listened to Joey at the Ghost Show. He clenched a fist and tried. There were dozens of people.

"Step up! Step up!" he called. "Living pictures!"

No good. His voice sounded terrible, thin and reedy.

"You must look cheerful," Joey had told him.

Snivel didn't feel cheerful but he screwed up his face and did his best, putting on a forced grin. "Laa-dies and gennel-men!"

This time he yelled. People outside the Fat Lady tent turned to look. His voice grew stronger. He caught sight of the wording on the notice board.

"See a modern miracle . . . Living pictures . . . Pictures that walk. Hurry in now . . . "

He was startled as a man and a woman moved past. A moment later others began to follow into the tent. It was working!

Henry had set up the limelight. He had loaded the calcium onto its holder. Nothing must go wrong.

Jenny waved urgently. "Henry, we're full!" She struggled to close the flap. Twelve people were inside and more were at the entrance.

"Sorry," she told them. "We've no more room just yet."

Henry took a deep breath. They were ready. He cleared his throat.

"Ladies and gentlemen," he declared. "A special announcement."

Every face turned his way.

"Welcome! This is our first show! You are our first audience and because we are late we don't want you to pay!"

Laughter and cheers greeted him.

Quickly Henry lit the gas nozzles.

A blaze of limelight hit the screen.

"Goodness!"

Jenny was taken by surprise.

Henry started to crank the projector handle.

For a moment the screen was blank then astonished cries filled the tent. The screen suddenly was full of pictures of people streaming out of a factory entrance.

"Wow!" gasped Snivel.

Jenny could hardly believe her eyes.

"Look at the women's hats! And their clothes!"

Everyone was talking.

Henry kept on cranking. Never had he imagined anything this exciting. Magically the factory workers vanished, and in their place appeared a couple sitting feeding a baby. The audience clapped delightedly.

It was miraculous. Even the baby was moving!

Film followed film: a wall being knocked down; men playing cards at a table; and suddenly a film of a gardener watering the garden. Henry recognised it at once. It was the bit he had seen at Kendal, but now it was the whole film. A boy stood with a foot on the hosepipe and the gardener stared down the nozzle wondering where the water had gone. Wickedly the boy removed his foot.

A roar of laughter and squeals filled the tent as the hose jerked to life and squirted the man in the face.

Still more laughs greeted the sudden arrival of a belly dancer – *Fatima's Dance*, labelled For *Gentlemen's Smoking Concerts only*; and then the last shot.

A train came steaming towards them! A shining monster. It was gliding into the tent. With a scream a woman at the front tried to scramble clear and was still struggling as the gleaming engine hurtled past and disappeared.

Pandemonium! The tent was full of excited voices. A moment later it filled with applause.

"Nay, lad, that were really summat!" cried an old man, as the audience left. "Living pictures!"

Henry gulped. It had been a close thing. Too close!

Snivel bounced up and down. "Did ya see 'em? Even their mouths was moving!"

"Come on, let's get on with the next show," said Jenny enthusiastically.

Performance after performance followed. As fast as the tent could be emptied and the film rewound the next audience crowded in. All day they went on and not until nine o'clock at night was striking did they stop. All three were exhausted.

Jenny added up the takings.

Ninety people at a penny each, and twenty-four children at a ha-penny . . .

Phew! She could hardly believe it.

"We've taken eight shillings and sixpence!" she told them.

"Wow!"

"Crikey!"

A fortune!

Jenny said: "It's brilliant. But what do we do now?"

"We write down a list of places," said Henry. His voice rang with confidence. "We'll go everywhere! Carlisle, Kendal, Ulverston, wherever we can find fairs . . . Everyone's going to want to see living pictures. I know they are."

He was excited. There was no knowing where they would go! Film show pioneers.

41

Something Important

Henry glanced at Snivel. Late though it was, now was the moment. He gave him a knowing nod. "Sniv-sorry . . . Freddy, er . . ."

Sniv got the message and gave a toothy grin. "Oh, I'll just go and see how Bellow's doing. I bet he's hungry."

"Would you?" Jenny smiled, happy and tired.

Snivel went out.

Henry coughed. "Jen . . . there's something I want to ask you, something important, I mean."

His eyes met hers.

He cleared his throat. "It's . . . that is, I mean . . ."

Jenny grew very quiet. She knew what she was going to say. She was going to say yes.

The Biddall's Ghost Show

George Biddall's Ghost Show was one of the most popular travelling shows in the last decades of the 19th century. For some sixty years its ghostly wails haunted fairgrounds across the North of England, attracting fascinated crowds, particularly at the spring and autumn hirings.

The poorer Cumbrian people had a real affection for the Biddall family, and especially for George. He was a generous spirited man and greatly liked, giving among other things free shows to workhouse inmates. In the fairground world he was held in high esteem and regarded by many as one of the finest men to travel the roads.

George Biddall on the road with his Ghost Show © University of Sheffield National Fairground Archive

While the North was the Ghost Show's main haunting ground, George also travelled into the Borders with his ghosts – and later he and members of his family presented fairground shows of the recently invented, and equally astonishing moving picture shows.

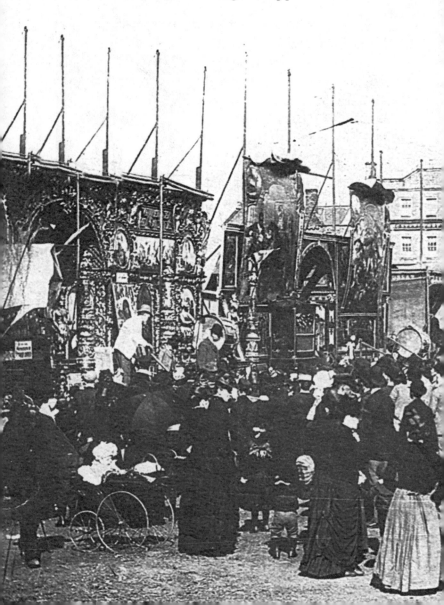

He was not the only Biddall on the roads. His father had been there before him; and there were other successful Biddall fairground enterprises throughout the country whose stories are well told in *Fairground Strollers and Showfolk* by Frances Brown.

George lived until 1909 and like his wife Selina ended his days in Cockermouth, a town both of them loved. Today the original fearsome ghost slumbers in the Beacon Museum in Whitehaven, emerging at times from layers of tissue to stare hauntingly at visitors.

The origins of the ghostly illusions go back to the 1860s, when it was popularised and named after John Henry Pepper. George was among the many showmen who made the shows famous.

Fairground crowd at the Sands, Carlisle. Circa 1900.

An early Eragraph projector